Katusha

Girl Soldier of the Great Patriotic War

Wayne Vansant

THE SHAKING OF THE EARTH

GRAND DESIGN
PUBLISHING

Susan Barrows – Copy Editor and Computer Support
Fabrice Sapolsky – Additional design
David Bernstein – Publisher

For foreign rights information please contact
David Bernstein : granddesignagent@gmail.com.

Published by Grand Design Publishing, a division of Grand Design
Communications.

www.granddesignonline.net
facebook.com/granddesigncommunications
facebook.com/katushagraphicnovel

Printed in the USA.
December 2013.

THE SHAKING OF THE EARTH

Words & Pictures by **Wayne Vansant**

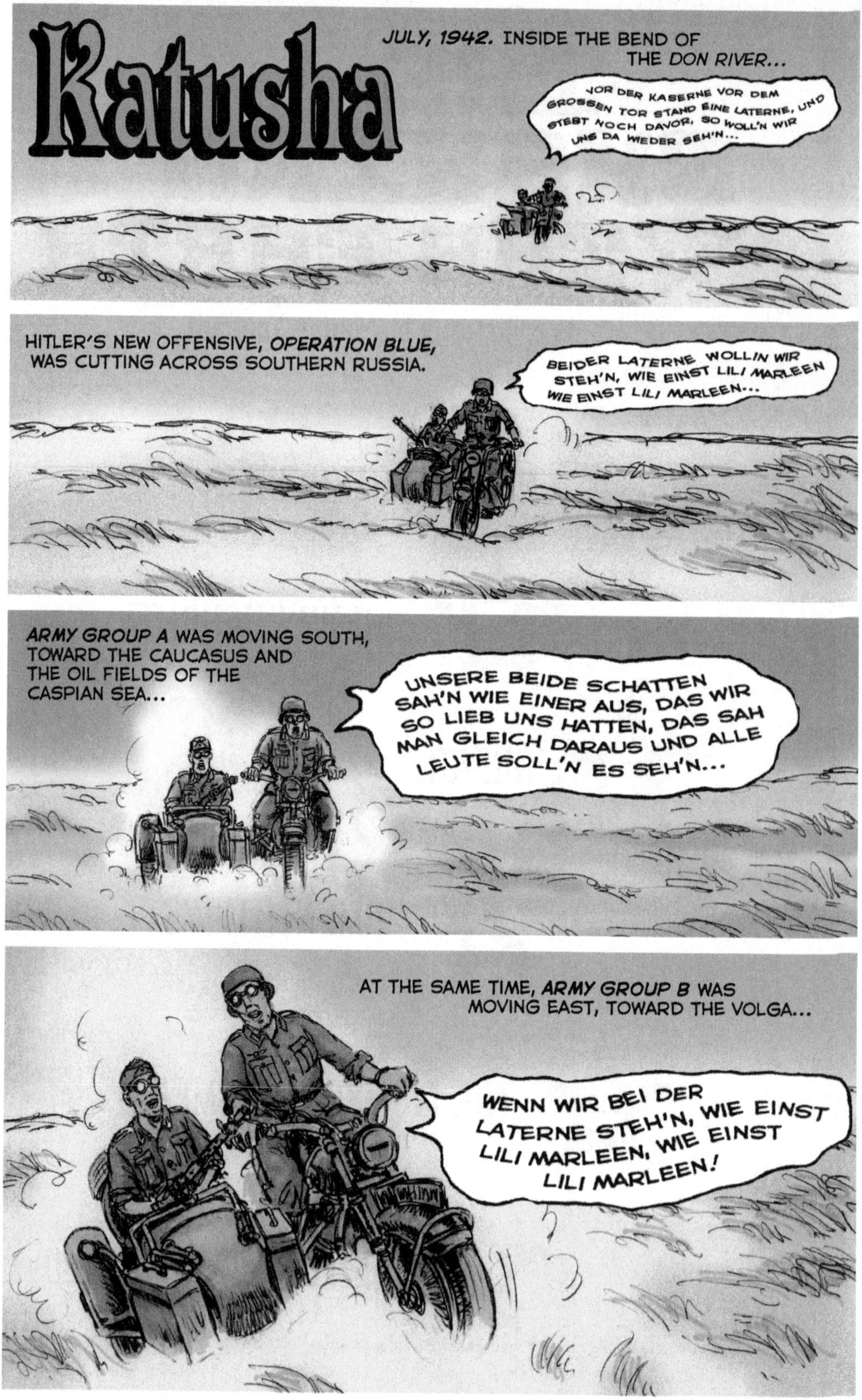
Katusha
JULY, 1942. INSIDE THE BEND OF THE DON RIVER...
VOR DER KASERNE VOR DEM GROSSEN TOR STAND EINE LATERNE, UND STEBT NOCH DAVOR, SO WOLL'N WIR UNS DA WIEDER SEH'N...
HITLER'S NEW OFFENSIVE, OPERATION BLUE, WAS CUTTING ACROSS SOUTHERN RUSSIA.
BEIDER LATERNE WOLLIN WIR STEH'N, WIE EINST LILI MARLEEN WIE EINST LILI MARLEEN...
ARMY GROUP A WAS MOVING SOUTH, TOWARD THE CAUCASUS AND THE OIL FIELDS OF THE CASPIAN SEA...
UNSERE BEIDE SCHATTEN SAH'N WIE EINER AUS, DAS WIR SO LIEB UNS HATTEN, DAS SAH MAN GLEICH DARAUS UND ALLE LEUTE SOLL'N ES SEH'N...
AT THE SAME TIME, ARMY GROUP B WAS MOVING EAST, TOWARD THE VOLGA...
WENN WIR BEI DER LATERNE STEH'N, WIE EINST LILI MARLEEN, WIE EINST LILI MARLEEN!

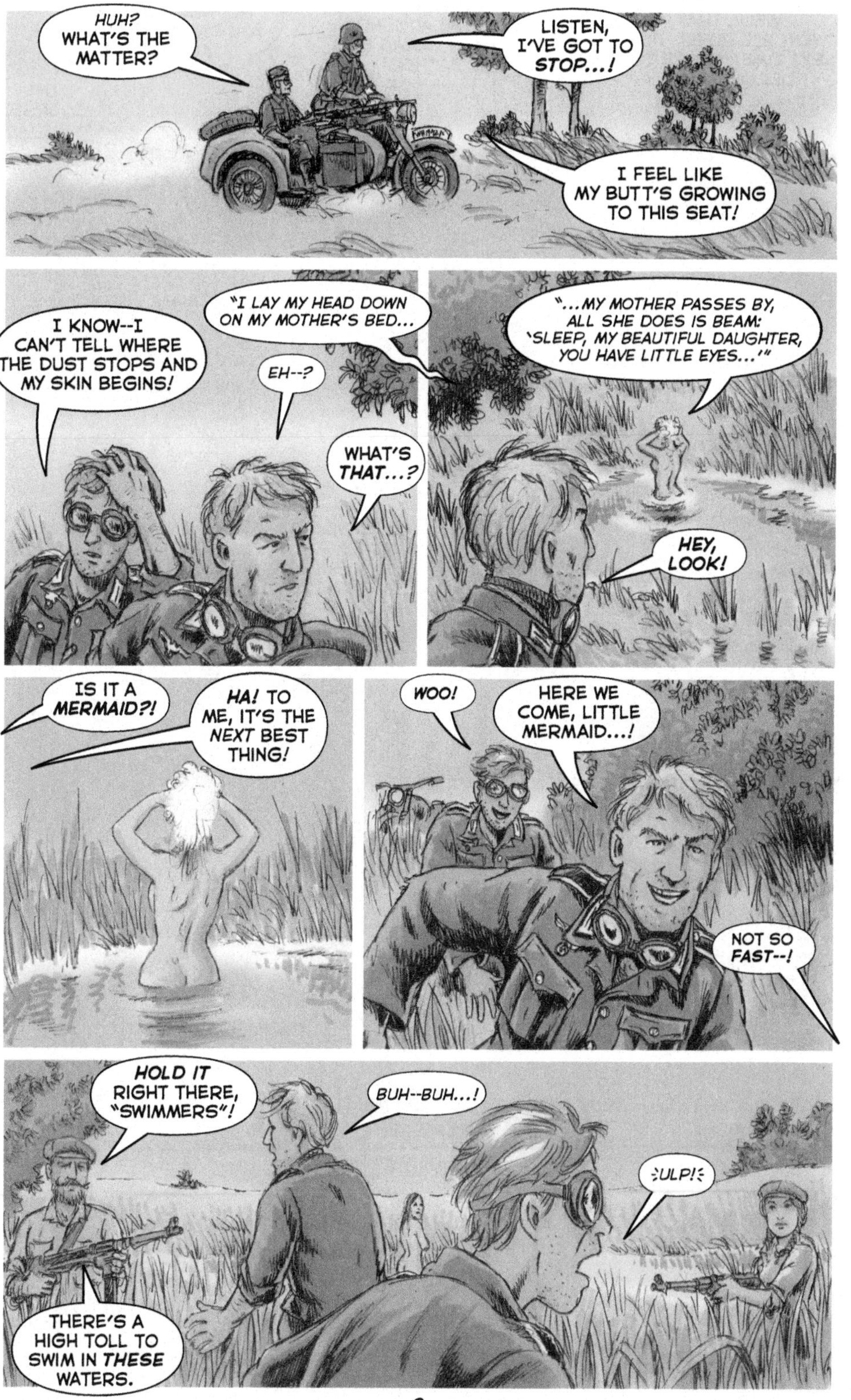
HUH? WHAT'S THE MATTER?
LISTEN, I'VE GOT TO STOP...!
I FEEL LIKE MY BUTT'S GROWING TO THIS SEAT!
I KNOW--I CAN'T TELL WHERE THE DUST STOPS AND MY SKIN BEGINS!
"I LAY MY HEAD DOWN ON MY MOTHER'S BED...
EH--?
WHAT'S THAT...?
"...MY MOTHER PASSES BY, ALL SHE DOES IS BEAM: 'SLEEP, MY BEAUTIFUL DAUGHTER, YOU HAVE LITTLE EYES...'"
HEY, LOOK!
IS IT A MERMAID?!
HA! TO ME, IT'S THE NEXT BEST THING!
WOO!
HERE WE COME, LITTLE MERMAID...!
NOT SO FAST--!
HOLD IT RIGHT THERE, "SWIMMERS"!
BUH--BUH...!
ULP!
THERE'S A HIGH TOLL TO SWIM IN THESE WATERS.

WELL, THAT WENT ALL RIGHT--BUT NEXT TIME, *YOU* BE THE DECOY, MILLA!

I KNOW-- NEXT TIME AROUND, WE'LL LET *TARAS* BE THE BATHER!

OH, YES! HEE HEE HEE..!

UH-HUH. HA, HA.

OKAY, LET'S HIT THE ROAD...CAN YOU DRIVE THIS THING ALL RIGHT?

OF COURSE!

OH, YEAH...

I ALMOST *FORGOT* ABOUT YOU TWO...!

I TURNED MY HEAD. I KNEW THAT YOU DARED NOT SHOW MERCY TODAY TO SOMEONE WHO WOULD SURELY *NOT* SHOW MERCY TO YOU TOMORROW.

I UNDERSTOOD THIS PERFECTLY...

...BUT I DIDN'T HAVE TO *LIKE* IT.

3

NOT ONE STEP BACK!
AS WE MOVED EASTWARD, WE RAN INTO MORE AND MORE RED ARMY UNITS. ALL WERE TIRED, HUNGRY, AND DISILLUSIONED. NONE OF THEM TRIED TO CHECK UP ON US, AND WE WEREN'T BOTHERED WITH SECURITY MATTERS UNTIL WE REACHED THE DON RIVER CROSSING AT NIZHNIY-CHIRSKAYA. BY THEN, OUR MOTORCYCLE HAD LONG SINCE RUN OUT OF GAS AND HAD BEEN ABANDONED.
...AND I'M AFRAID WE HAVE NO IDENTIFICATION ON US...
UKRAINIAN PARTISANS, EH? I'D SAY YOU WERE FAR OUT OF YOUR TERRITORY--THE TITLE NO LONGER FITS.
IF YOU'RE EXPECTING HARASSMENT FROM ME, YOU CAN FORGET IT...
THE "BOSS" HAS PUT OUT THE WORD--*NO ONE* IS TO BE ALLOWED TO PASS THE *VOLGA*.
"*NOT ONE STEP BACK!*" HE HAS ORDERED.

WELL! THAT WAS A SURPRISE--HE SEEMED LIKE A PRETTY DECENT FELLOW...!

I KNOW-- ESPECIALLY FOR AN *NKVD* MAN.

LOOK AT THIS!

WHAT *IS* IT, UNCLE TARAS--?

WHY, THAT IS A *CAMEL*, KATUSHA!

HE'S A RATHER UGLY CREATURE, ISN'T HE?

WELL, I THINK HE'S *CUTE*!

OH, I WOULDN'T SAY THA--

GROONNNKH!!

AAGKH!!

WELL, SO MUCH FOR *BEAUTY*!

WE SPENT THAT NIGHT IN A LITTLE SHACK BESIDE THE ROAD. IT WAS THE HOME OF AN OLD WOMAN WHOSE DAUGHTER HAD RUN AWAY LONG AGO.

HAVING MILLA AND ME THERE SEEMED TO SOOTHE HER BROKEN HEART. SHE FED US A WONDERFUL THIN MILLET SOUP, AND THEN WE BEDDED DOWN FOR THE NIGHT...

UNCLE TARAS--DO YOU THINK WE'LL EVER GET TO GO HOME AGAIN?

OF COURSE YOU WILL! *I* CAME HOME AGAIN, DIDN'T I?

I *KNOW* YOU DID, BUT IT TOOK OVER *TWENTY YEARS!*

...AND I DON'T WANT TO BE... *OH*, YOU KNOW --*OLD!*

HA! SO *THAT'S* IT, THEN...!

THE FUTURE'S FULL OF MYSTERY. PERHAPS THE GERMANS WILL PUSH US BACK AS FAR AS THEY WANT--AND THEN TRY MAKING PEACE.

WHO KNOWS...? MAYBE THE GERMANS WILL TAKE *ALL* SOVIET TERRITORIES...! BUT, THEN AGAIN--MAYBE STALIN WILL *WIN.*

EITHER WAY, LIFE WILL BE *HARD*-- BUT IT *ALWAYS* IS.

WE MOVED EAST ALL SUMMER, AND AS WE WENT, THE ROAD BECAME MORE AND MORE CROWDED. THE PACE ALSO BECAME MORE FRANTIC, BECAUSE THE GERMANS WERE CATCHING UP WITH US. "MEDDERS" STRAFING THE ROADS BECAME AN EVERYDAY EXPERIENCE. BUT WHEN WE REALIZED WE WERE WITHIN RANGE OF THEIR HEAVY ARTILLERY, WE KNEW THAT THE ROAD HAD ALMOST COME TO AN END...

...AND THE ROAD CERTAINLY WAS WELL MARKED.

▶ Сталинград ▶

STALINGRAD.

...ORIGINALLY CALLED *TSARITSYN,* IT WAS RENAMED IN *1925* TO HONOR OUR ILLUSTRIOUS LEADER. IT IS A CITY OF HEAVY INDUSTRY AND SHIPPING, WITH RAIL CONNECTIONS TO EVERY POINT ON THE COMPASS!

THIS LOVELY CITY OF PARKS AND BROAD STREETS IS HOME TO 500,000 CITIZEN WORKERS--

UH-OH--!

OH, *NO!* I HEAR IT, *TOO--!*

IT WAS *SUNDAY, AUGUST 23,* A DAY THAT I WILL NEVER FORGET. AS THE SUN ROSE OVER THE VOLGA, WAVES AND WAVES OF JUNKERS AND HEINKELS CAME TO MEET IT.

ON THIS DAY, THE MODEL CITY OF *STALINGRAD,* WITH ITS TALL, WHITE APARTMENT BUILDINGS AND LONG, TREE-LINED BOULEVARDS...

...WOULD BECOME A *HELL ON EARTH.*

THE GERMANS BOMBED NOT ONLY THE INDUSTRIAL TARGETS, BUT *EVERYTHING.* ALL OF THE ABLE-BODIED MEN HAD GONE INTO SERVICE--IT WAS A CITY OF OLD FOLKS, WOMEN, AND CHILDREN, LEFT WITH NO OPTION BUT TO HIDE IN THE SLIT TRENCHES THEY'D DUG IN THEIR GARDENS, IN CELLARS, OR IN THE RAVINES THAT RAN DOWN TO THE RIVER...

STALIN HADN'T ALLOWED AN EVACUATION--HE BELIEVED HIS SOLDIERS WOULD FIGHT MORE FIERCELY FOR A *LIVING* CITY THAN A *DEAD* ONE.

WHEN THE HUGE PETROLEUM TANK ON THE BANKS OF THE RIVER WAS HIT, A COLOSSAL *FIREBALL* ROSE 1,500 FEET INTO THE AIR.

FOR DAYS, THE ANGRY COLUMNS OF BLACK SMOKE COULD BE SEEN FROM TWO HUNDRED MILES AWAY...

IT WAS *WHOLESALE OBLITERATION.* ENTIRE NEIGHBORHOODS DISAPPEARED AS THEIR BUILDINGS, STREETS, AND PEOPLE MERGED INTO A NIGHTMARE OF CHARRED RUBBLE.

INCENDIARY BOMBS FELL ON THE WOODEN HOUSES OF THE SOUTHWESTERN PART OF THE CITY, TURNING THE DISTRICT INTO AN EERIE GRAVEYARD OF STONE AND BRICK CHIMNEYS.

PERHAPS AS MANY AS *40,000* OF ITS CITIZENS *DIED* IN THIS OPENING BOMBARDMENT.

NEAR US WERE *37MM* ANTI-AIRCRAFT GUNS-- MANNED BY YOUNG GIRLS, MANY OF THEM NO OLDER THAN I WAS.

LET'S GIVE THEM A HAND!

AT LEAST WE CAN PASS THEM AMMUNITION.

HOW CAN WE HELP?

THE AMMO BUNKER'S RIGHT THERE. IF THERE ARE ENOUGH OF YOU, YOU CAN PASS IT LIKE A BUCKET BRIGADE.

AH! THERE WE GO, ALL *DONE!*

NO MORE TARGETS FOR NOW. *NOW,* WE GET A *BREAK!*

I DON'T THINK SO! DON'T YOU HEAR THAT *NOISE--?*

THAT SOUND WAS ONE I'D HEARD BEFORE--AND DREADED HEARING AGAIN. OUT OF THE SMOKE EMERGED GERMAN *PANZER IVs!*

THE *16TH PANZER DIVISION* HAD ARRIVED AT STALINGRAD.

THE BATTERY COMMANDER, WHO'D TAUGHT SCHOOL IN STALINGRAD BEFORE THE WAR, REACTED QUICKLY...!

KEEP THAT *AMMO* COMING!

CRANK THOSE *GUNS* DOWN TO ZERO DEGREES--AND *OPEN FIRE--!!*

THE *37MM* ROUNDS FAILED TO PENETRATE THE ARMOR OF THE TANKS UNLESS THE RANGE WAS ALMOST *POINT BLANK.*

THEY COULD, HOWEVER, KNOCK OFF A TRACK OR EVEN OPEN A HATCH, IF LUCKY.

DESPITE ONLY MINOR SUCCESSES, THE GIRL GUNNERS KEPT AT IT...

...EVEN WHEN THE GERMAN GUNS WERE TAKING THEM OUT AT A GREATER DISTANCE.

THE GERMAN TANKERS WERE *STUNNED* TO REALIZE THAT THE GUNS WERE MANNED BY YOUNG GIRLS...!

I SUPPOSE THEY'D NEVER HEARD THE OLD MYTH OF THE *SARMATAE* OF THE LOWER VOLGA, A RACE OF FEMALE WARRIORS WHO WERE SAID TO BE DESCENDED FROM THE *SCYTHIANS* AND THE LEGENDARY *AMAZONS.*

WE STUMBLED THROUGH THE FIERY RUBBLE, LOOKING FOR SOME ORGANIZATION TO ATTACH OURSELVES TO. SOME *NKVD* MEN WERE PATCHING TOGETHER GROUPS OF STRAGGLERS INTO SMALL *AD HOC* UNITS FOR DEFENSE...

AH, YOU THREE--!

HMM...REPORT TO THE DZERZHINSKY TRACTOR FACTORY. A MILITIA UNIT IS BEING FORMED THERE.

GOOD! A MILITIA IS A STEP UP FROM PARTISANS-- OH, BY THE WAY...

...WHAT HAPPENED TO THE *NKVD* MEN AT THE NIZHNIY-CHIRSKAYA BRIDGE?

THEY *DIED* DEFENDING THE BRIDGE...

...EVERY LAST ONE OF THEM.

WE FOUND THE DZERZHINSKY TRACTOR FACTORY. THOUGH DAMAGED IN THE BOMBING, IT WAS STILL BUZZING WITH ACTIVITY.

THEY BUILD *T-34* TANKS HERE!

AMONG MANY OTHER PLACES, I UNDERSTAND...

INSIDE, EVERYTHING WAS CLICKING AND SPINNING ALONG WITH ORGANIZED CHAOS...

SOME OF THE MACHINERY IS BEING DISASSEMBLED BY THE TECHNICIANS, TO BE SENT TO THE FACTORIES EAST OF THE URALS...

STILL, WE INTEND TO CONTINUE OUR OPERATIONS HERE, COME WHAT MAY...

WHILE TARAS TALKED TO THE WORKER, I WANDERED AWAY INTO THE HUGE FACTORY THAT RATTLED AND CLANKED WITH ACTIVITY. IT WAS NOT A MODERN PLACE LIKE DPECHERSK OR BANKIVSKA, BUT ITS SENSIBLE DESIGN AND DEDICATION TO PURPOSE REPRESENTED A CERTAIN KIND OF BEAUTY.

I THEN NOTICED A MAN WHOSE *BACK* SEEMED SOMEHOW FAMILIAR TO ME...

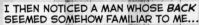

?

PAPA...?

EH--?

AH!!

IT WAS A MOST JOYOUS AND UNEXPECTED REUNION, ESPECIALLY BETWEEN MY FATHER AND UNCLE TARAS. THEIR PURE AND UNINTERRUPTED LOVE FOR EACH OTHER WAS SO OBVIOUS IT WAS ALL I COULD DO TO KEEP FROM CRYING AND SPOILING THE EVENT.

11

PAPA'S SUPERIORS, WHO OBVIOUSLY MUST HAVE RESPECTED HIM A GREAT DEAL, LET US USE AN EMPTY OFFICE IN A CORNER OF THE FACTORY. THERE WE TALKED AND CAUGHT UP UNTIL LATE AT NIGHT.

PAPA WAS CONCERNED AND UPSET ABOUT HOW OUR FAMILY HAD BEEN SCATTERED FAR AND WIDE. BUT CONSIDERING THE TIMES, HE WAS STILL GRATEFUL IT HAD TURNED OUT AS WELL AS IT HAD. HE WAS GLAD THAT WE HAD THUS FAR PREVAILED, AND HE HOPED THAT OUR APPARENT GOOD FORTUNE WOULD SEE US THROUGH.

AS WE SPENT THIS TIME TOGETHER, HE SEEMED TO DETECT THE CONNECTION BETWEEN TARAS AND MILLA. AT FIRST, HE SEEMED AS IF IT BOTHERED HIM A BIT--BUT I COULD SEE HIM GRADUALLY REACH A QUIET ACCEPTANCE.

MILLA AND I HAD FINALLY BECOME SO TIRED FROM OUR JOURNEY THAT WE JUST HAD TO SLEEP.

THE LAST THING I REMEMBER BEFORE CLOSING MY EYES WAS UNCLE TARAS AND PAPA TALKING QUIETLY AND VERY SERIOUSLY IN A CORNER OF THE ROOM...

THE FIRST THING I NOTICED AS I AWOKE THE NEXT MORNING WAS THE SOUND OF SMALL-ARMS AND ARTILLERY FIRE IN THE DISTANCE.

⸮YAAAWN⸮

⸮SIGH⸮ ALREADY AT IT, I SEE...

WHERE'S PAPA?

HE'LL BE BACK SOON.

HE WENT TO SPEAK WITH A POLITICAL OFFICER WHO OWES HIM A FAVOR.

BY THE TIME PAPA GOT BACK, WE WERE ALL UP AND MUNCHING ON SOME MOSTLY UNMOLDY BREAD. PAPA WAS CARRYING A BROWN ENVELOPE AND WORE A LOOK OF SATISFACTION...

ALL RIGHT!

WE ARE GETTING YOU GIRLS *OUT* OF STALINGRAD!

I WAS IMMEDIATELY CURIOUS... BUT *MILLA'S* EXPRESSION--?

--PURE *SUSPICION.*

WELL, YOUR FATHER AND I TALKED IT OVER LAST NIGHT, AND IT MAKES *SENSE.* THE FIGHT HERE IN THE CITY IS GOING TO BE BAD, AND IF THE GERMANS MANAGE TO *TAKE* STALINGRAD AND CUT THE VOLGA--THAT WILL JUST ABOUT FINISH THE WAR FOR *US.*

FOR THE TIME BEING, WE WOULD LIKE TO THINK THAT THE BOTH OF YOU ARE *SAFE.*

THE SENIOR POLITICAL COMMISSAR HERE OWES ME ONE--HE'S ALSO UKRAINIAN. HE'S PROVIDED ME WITH ALL THE TRAVEL PERMITS AND INTRODUCTIONS THAT YOU'LL NEED-- BECAUSE YOU GIRLS ARE GOING TO *CHELYABINSK...*

...TO ENTER THE *TANK-DRIVING SCHOOL.*

THE IDEA GAVE ME A RUSH OF EXCITEMENT--! BUT WHEN I LOOKED OVER AT MILLA TO GAUGE HER REACTION, HER EXPRESSION WAS ONE OF *HURT...*EVEN *BETRAYAL.*

SILENTLY, SHE TURNED AND STRODE OUT OF THE ROOM.

13

UNCLE TARAS WENT RIGHT AFTER HER...

PAPA, I THINK YOU DESERVE AN EXPLANATION ABOUT--

KATUSHA, I HAVE ALL THE EXPLANATION I NEED. LUDMILLA IS A GROWN WOMAN...

...AND SO ARE *YOU.*

THAT EVENING, PAPA AND UNCLE TARAS SAW US OFF AT THE RIVER DOCKS, WHERE A FERRY WOULD CARRY US ACROSS THE VOLGA. IT WAS A VERY DIFFICULT PARTING FOR ALL OF US, FOR OUR FAMILY WAS FRAGMENTING YET AGAIN.

THE CROSSING WOULD BE MORE DIFFICULT YET. AN ATTACK WAS IN PROGRESS.

GERMAN ARTILLERY AND PLANES RAINED DOWN A CONSTANT BARRAGE OF HORRIFIC DESTRUCTION.

A BARGE LOADED WITH WOUNDED WAS HIT AND SUNK RIGHT BESIDE US!

WHEN WE REACHED THE OTHER SIDE, I LOOKED BACK ACROSS AT THE CITY--AND WENT NUMB WITH HORROR. STALINGRAD FLASHED AND ROARED LIKE HELL ITSELF, THE FIERY LIGHT REFLECTING ON THE RIVER'S SURFACE MAKING THE VOLGA LOOK LIKE *BLOOD.*

WE WALKED SEVERAL MILES TO WHERE WE WERE TO CATCH OUR TRAIN. APPARENTLY OUR PAPERWORK WAS IMPECCABLE, SINCE EVERY *NKVD* MAN WHO SAW IT WENT ALL WIDE-EYED AND POLITELY PASSED US RIGHT THROUGH.

WE RODE IN A CATTLE CAR PACKED WITH ALL TYPES OF PEOPLE...

BUT NO UNIFORMED SOLDIERS WERE AMONG US. THEY'D ALL BEEN LEFT BEHIND FOR THE FIGHT TO *DEFEND STALINGRAD.*

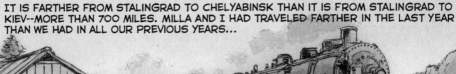

IT IS FARTHER FROM STALINGRAD TO CHELYABINSK THAN IT IS FROM STALINGRAD TO KIEV--MORE THAN 700 MILES. MILLA AND I HAD TRAVELED FARTHER IN THE LAST YEAR THAN WE HAD IN ALL OUR PREVIOUS YEARS...

...NOT THAT THERE HAD BEEN THAT MANY YET.

AFTER THREE DAYS' TRAVEL, WE REACHED *CHELYABINSK* DURING THE NIGHT. SECURITY WAS TIGHT...

THE *NKVD* OFFICERS WANTED TO TAKE OUR WEAPONS--BUT ONE LOOK AT OUR PAPERS, AND *THEIR* EYES GOT LIKE SAUCERS AND THEY LET US PASS, *ARMED.*

ALL THIS WAS BEGINNING TO BE SUCH A FAMILIAR ROUTINE WE'D STARTED TO WONDER--WHAT *WAS* IT ABOUT THE SIGNATURE OF THIS *"NIKITA SERGEYEVICH KHRUSHCHEV,"* ANYWAY?

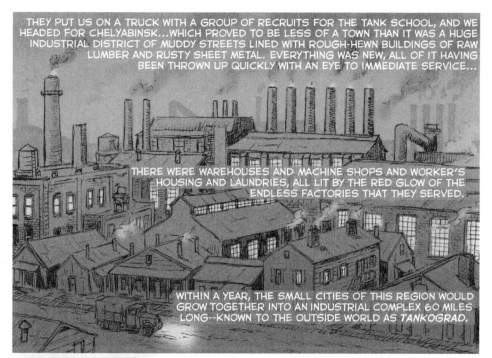

THEY PUT US ON A TRUCK WITH A GROUP OF RECRUITS FOR THE TANK SCHOOL, AND WE HEADED FOR CHELYABINSK...WHICH PROVED TO BE LESS OF A TOWN THAN IT WAS A HUGE INDUSTRIAL DISTRICT OF MUDDY STREETS LINED WITH ROUGH-HEWN BUILDINGS OF RAW LUMBER AND RUSTY SHEET METAL. EVERYTHING WAS NEW, ALL OF IT HAVING BEEN THROWN UP QUICKLY WITH AN EYE TO IMMEDIATE SERVICE...

THERE WERE WAREHOUSES AND MACHINE SHOPS AND WORKER'S HOUSING AND LAUNDRIES, ALL LIT BY THE RED GLOW OF THE ENDLESS FACTORIES THAT THEY SERVED.

WITHIN A YEAR, THE SMALL CITIES OF THIS REGION WOULD GROW TOGETHER INTO AN INDUSTRIAL COMPLEX 60 MILES LONG--KNOWN TO THE OUTSIDE WORLD AS *TANKOGRAD*.

THE TRUCK PULLED UP IN FRONT OF A LONG, SQUAT BUILDING, WHERE WE WERE GREETED WITH SHOUTED CURSES FROM A WOMAN SERGEANT.

SHE DIRECTED US INTO A LONG HALL, WHERE WE STOOD IN A ROW WHILE A PALE POLITICAL OFFICER LED US IN RECITING AN OATH TO DEFEND OUR *MOTHER RUSSIA*...

THEN A KISS OF ALLEGIANCE TO THE FLAG-- AND WE WERE OFFICIALLY PART OF THE *RED ARMY.*

THEY GAVE US BAGS SORT OF LIKE GRAIN SACKS FOR ANY PERSONAL ITEMS WE WISHED TO KEEP. MILLA AND I STUCK OUR WEAPONS IN THESE TO MINIMIZE THE CURIOUS LOOKS WE WERE GETTING.

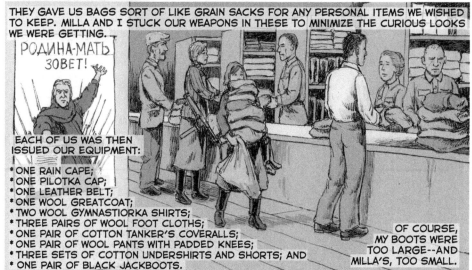

РОДИНА-МАТЬ ЗОВЕТ!

EACH OF US WAS THEN ISSUED OUR EQUIPMENT:

* ONE RAIN CAPE;
* ONE PILOTKA CAP;
* ONE LEATHER BELT;
* ONE WOOL GREATCOAT;
* TWO WOOL GYMNASTIORKA SHIRTS;
* THREE PAIRS OF WOOL FOOT CLOTHS;
* ONE PAIR OF COTTON TANKER'S COVERALLS;
* ONE PAIR OF WOOL PANTS WITH PADDED KNEES;
* THREE SETS OF COTTON UNDERSHIRTS AND SHORTS; AND
* ONE PAIR OF BLACK JACKBOOTS.

OF COURSE, MY BOOTS WERE TOO LARGE--AND MILLA'S, TOO SMALL.

WE WERE LED TO A SHOWER ROOM WITH A CONCRETE FLOOR.

THE WATER WAS BARELY LUKEWARM, BUT WHAT A BLESSING IT WAS...!

IT FELT GREAT TO WASH OFF A FEW HUNDRED MILES OF DIRT.

AHH...!

WHEN IT CAME TO THE BARBER'S CHAIR, MILLA BACKED OFF...

TARAS LIKES MY HAIR LONG-- I'LL JUST BRAID IT.

I LONGED TO BE MORE ACCEPTING OF CHANGES IN MY LIFE, SO I PUT MYSELF AT THE MERCY OF THE BARBER. I COULD TELL HE WAS PROUD OF THE RESULTS.

I SMILED IN GRATITUDE... BUT DEEP INSIDE, I *CRIED.*

THEY THEN DROPPED US OFF IN FRONT OF A SIMPLE WOODEN BARRACKS WHICH SEEMED TO BE FLOATING IN A SEA OF MUD.

UNFORTUNATELY, IT WAS LATE WHEN WE GOT IN, SO WE WERE ASSIGNED THE LAST TWO BUNKS AVAILABLE.

WE WALKED INTO A SOLID WALL OF NOISE AS EVERYONE WAS GETTING UP FOR THE DAY.

NEVER HAVE I HEARD SO MUCH CURSING FROM THE MOUTHS OF WOMEN...! WITHIN MOMENTS, I HAD HEARD GOD'S NAME BLASPHEMED IN EVERY LANGUAGE AND DIALECT OF THE SOVIET UNION.

WE WERE LINED UP OUTSIDE AND MARCHED TO BREAKFAST...

...SOMETHING MILLA AND I WERE *NOT* VERY GOOD AT.

IT SEEMED ODD TO ME HOW EVERYBODY COMPLAINED ABOUT THE FOOD. I THOUGHT BREAKFAST WAS PRETTY GOOD--PORRIDGE, MEAT, AND BREAD WITH BUTTER.

SO...YOU'RE THE *TYMOSHENKO SISTERS, EH?*

YOU SURE DON'T *LOOK* LIKE SISTERS...

WELL, WE *ARE.*

HEY, YURI! WHAT DO YOU THINK WAS IN THOSE *AWFUL* SAUSAGES--?

:UGH: *BOOTS,* DEFINITELY. *OLD* ONES.

WORD IS YOU TWO SHOWED UP PACKING GERMAN WEAPONS--!

THAT'S TRUE.

WHERE WE'RE FROM, IT *COULD* BE A BAD IDEA TO GO *UNARMED...*

THINGS ARE GETTING *UNPREDICTABLE--*

HOO! WOULDJA LISTEN TO THAT HICK *ACCENT?*

HAW HAW!!

YEAH--LOOKS LIKE WE'RE SHARIN' BUNKS WITH A COUPLE OF *"TUFTIES"!**

I'M MARUSYA POZHARSKY.

OH, AND *DON'T* MIND THEM.

* RUDE TERM FOR A UKRAINIAN

MARUSYA, I WAS WONDERING. ALL THE OFFICERS ARE EATING TOGETHER-- EXCEPT FOR THAT ONE MAN, OVER BY THE WINDOW...

...WHY IS HE SITTING THERE ALL BY HIMSELF?

OH--THAT'S *CAPTAIN RAMSKOV.* HE TEACHES TANK-TO-TANK TACTICS...

YOU'LL MEET *HIM* LATER.

OUR SCHOOLING COMMENCED. ONE OF OUR INSTRUCTORS WE KNEW SIMPLY AS *SERGEANT TABOT* (GREASY).

WHEN FIRST DEVELOPED, THE *V-2 12-CYLINDER WATER-COOLED ENGINE* WAS BELIEVED TO COMPLETELY ELIMINATE ENGINE FIRES.

BUT THAT WAS BEFORE WE REALIZED THE TEMPERATURES GENERATED BY HIGH-VELOCITY ARMOR-PIERCING SHELLS! BELIEVE ME, WITH THE RIGHT CONDITIONS--

--A *T-34* WILL BURN LIKE A DRY HAYSTACK.

THE FOUR-STAGE TRANSMISSION WAS SO UNRELIABLE THAT A COMMON SIGHT WAS A *T-34* WITH A SPARE TRANSMISSION CHAINED TO ITS ENGINE DECK!

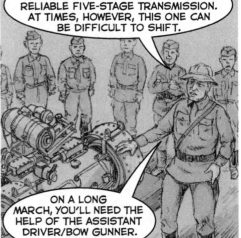

THE ANSWER WAS THIS MUCH MORE RELIABLE FIVE-STAGE TRANSMISSION. AT TIMES, HOWEVER, THIS ONE *CAN* BE DIFFICULT TO SHIFT.

ON A LONG MARCH, YOU'LL NEED THE HELP OF THE ASSISTANT DRIVER/BOW GUNNER.

I NEVER COULD HAVE MADE IT THROUGH THAT SCHOOL--

--IF IT HAD NOT BEEN FOR *MILLA.*

SHE HAD A CLEAR AND NATURAL UNDERSTANDING FOR MACHINERY THAT I DID NOT.

SHE MADE CHANGING OIL SEEM AS SIMPLE AS MILKING A COW...

...CLEANING AIR FILTERS JUST LIKE CHURNING BUTTER...

...REPLACING BRAKES LIKE SLIPPING ON A NEW PAIR OF SHOES...

...AND LUBRICATING PARTS JUST LIKE...

...LIKE...

...WELL, *YOU KNOW.*

THAT NIGHT, ALMOST AT "LIGHTS OUT"...

TYMOSHENKO TWINS...! CAPTAIN KOVCHENKO IS OUTSIDE AND REQUIRES YOUR PRESENCE!

"TWINS"-- VERY FUNNY.

SO...WHO IS KOVCHENKO?

WAITING FOR US OUTSIDE WERE THREE MEN. WHICH OF THEM WAS CAPTAIN KOVCHENKO WAS OBVIOUS--HE HAD THE LOOK OF A MAN NATURALLY BORN TO LEAD.

FLANKING HIM WERE A TALL, SKINNY SERGEANT AND A POLITICAL OFFICER WITH A DISAGREEABLE-LOOKING EXPRESSION ON HIS FACE.

COMRADES TYMOSHENKO-- IT HAS BEEN BROUGHT TO OUR ATTENTION THAT WHEN YOU ARRIVED HERE AT THE SCHOOL, YOU BOTH CARRIED WEAPONS OF ENEMY MANUFACTURE. PERSONAL WEAPONS ARE NOT ALLOWED IN THE BARRACKS--

--PARTICULARLY GERMAN WEAPONS.

COMRADE CAPTAIN, JUST WEEKS AGO, WE WERE PARTISANS. HAVING THOSE GUNS CLOSE BY MEANT OUR SURVIVAL. WITHOUT OUR WEAPONS--WE'D HAVE DIED A DOZEN TIMES OVER.

WE COULDN'T SLEEP A WINK WITHOUT THOSE GUNS BESIDE US.

THIS TIME, THE CAPTAIN SPOKE IN MILDER TONES...

COMRADES, WE'RE A LONG WAY FROM THE FRONT LINES.

THERE'S NO PLANE IN EXISTENCE THAT CAN BOMB US HERE. YOU ARE PERFECTLY SAFE.

FINALLY, I YIELDED.

VERY *WELL,* COMRADE CAPTAIN.

WE WILL GIVE YOU OUR WEAPONS.

MILLA AND I WENT INSIDE...

...AND CAME OUT BEARING A COLLECTION OF GUNS, KNIVES, GRENADES, AMMO...

VERY GOOD, COMRADE TYMOSHENKO. I TRUST YOU NOW FEEL ALL RIGHT ABOUT THIS.

HONESTLY, COMRADE CAPTAIN--

--I NOW FEEL *NAKED.*

WITH THIS LAST COMMENT, THE CAPTAIN LOOKED UP AT ME FROM UNDER HIS BILLED CAP...

...AND *SMILED* WARMLY.

HE THEN TURNED-- AND WALKED AWAY...!

EVEN IN THE MOONLIGHT, I COULD FEEL MY FACE GLOWING *SCARLET.*

WE WENT BACK INTO THE BARRACKS AND RIGHT INTO BED.

I DIDN'T SLEEP WELL THAT NIGHT...

...BUT IT HAD NOTHING TO DO WITH NOT HAVING A GUN BESIDE ME.

THE FINAL CLASS OF THE DAY WAS CAPTAIN RAMSKOV'S TANK TACTICS CLASS. MILLA AND I WERE THE LAST INTO THE ROOM, AND THE ONLY SEATS LEFT WERE UP AT THE FRONT.

THE CAPTAIN WAS WRITING ON THE BLACKBOARD--AND I COULD NOT HELP BUT NOTICE RIGHT AWAY THERE WAS SOMETHING *DIFFERENT* ABOUT HIM.

THEN...

...HE *TURNED AROUND.*

STUDENTS...!

...I LIKE TO BEGIN THIS CLASS WITH A QUESTION:

HOW MANY OFFENSIVE WEAPONS DOES THE *T-34* TANK POSSESS?

THREE, COMRADE CAPTAIN! A *76MM F-34 MSIN GUN* PLUS TWO *DT MACHINE GUNS*--WITH A TOTAL OF 2898 ROUNDS, ONE MOUNTED IN THE BOW AND ANOTHER CO-AXIALLY IN THE TURRET!

VERY GOOD! IS THERE ANYTHING ELSE?

YES, COMRADE CAPTAIN!

A *PPSH-43 SUBMACHINE GUN* IS ON BOARD IN CASE THE CREW MUST ABANDON THEIR TANK.

TRUE...

BUT YOU HAVE OVERLOOKED TWO OF THE *T-34'S MOST LETHAL* WEAPONS...

...THE TANK'S *TRACKS!* *NOTHING* CAN APPEAR MORE FEARSOME TO INFANTRY MEN THAN THE TANK'S DEADLY STEEL TRACKS!

IN THE *WINTER* MONTHS, WHEN THE GROUND IS FROZEN SOLID, THE ENEMY WILL BE FORCED TO DIG HIS FOXHOLES IN THE *SNOW.* IF YOU COME UPON A SOLDIER WHO IS DUG IN ONLY IN SNOW--

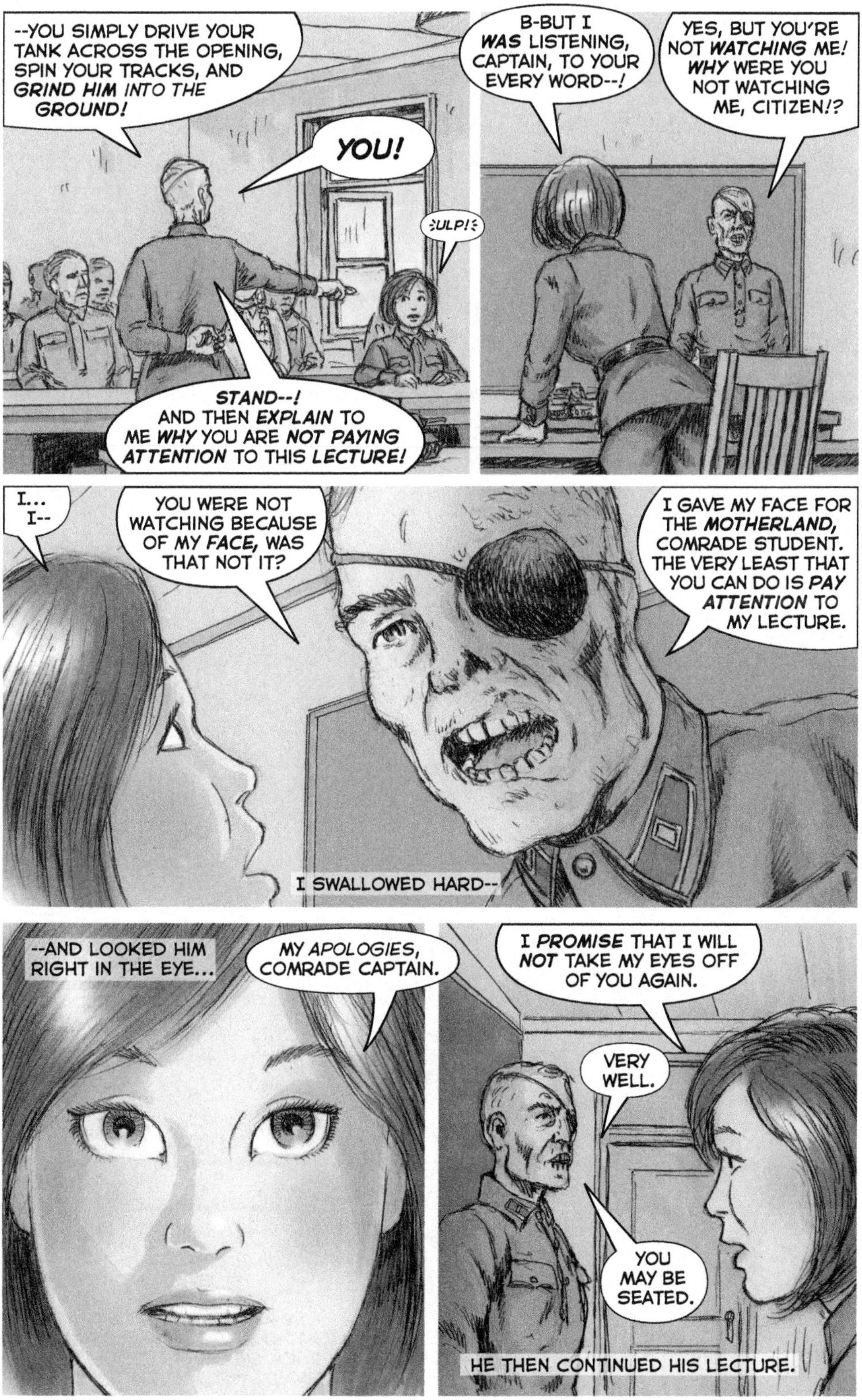
--YOU SIMPLY DRIVE YOUR TANK ACROSS THE OPENING, SPIN YOUR TRACKS, AND GRIND HIM INTO THE GROUND!
YOU!
ULP!
STAND--! AND THEN EXPLAIN TO ME WHY YOU ARE NOT PAYING ATTENTION TO THIS LECTURE!
B-BUT I WAS LISTENING, CAPTAIN, TO YOUR EVERY WORD--!
YES, BUT YOU'RE NOT WATCHING ME! WHY WERE YOU NOT WATCHING ME, CITIZEN!?
I... I--
YOU WERE NOT WATCHING BECAUSE OF MY FACE, WAS THAT NOT IT?
I GAVE MY FACE FOR THE MOTHERLAND, COMRADE STUDENT. THE VERY LEAST THAT YOU CAN DO IS PAY ATTENTION TO MY LECTURE.
I SWALLOWED HARD--
--AND LOOKED HIM RIGHT IN THE EYE...
MY APOLOGIES, COMRADE CAPTAIN.
I PROMISE THAT I WILL NOT TAKE MY EYES OFF OF YOU AGAIN.
VERY WELL.
YOU MAY BE SEATED.
HE THEN CONTINUED HIS LECTURE.

THE FIRST TIME I TRIED TO DRIVE A TANK, I WAS *EAGER.* I THOUGHT OF IT AS A FUN ADVENTURE.

WELL, *BIG* TYMOSHENKO DRIVES A TANK LIKE SHE WAS BORN TO IT!

NOW, LET'S SEE HOW *LITTLE* TYMOSHENKO DOES AT IT.

ALL *RIGHT.* NOW...

WHAT WAS IT MILLA TOLD ME...?

"JUST *EASE OUT* ON THE CLUTCH"--

WHOO!

⸮WHOOPS!⸮

WHOA--!!

I WAS SO SORE THAT NIGHT THAT MILLA HAD TO HELP ME INTO BED.

⸮UURNGHK!⸮

AT EASE, COMRADES. WE'RE JUST CHECKING ON OUR TRAINING IN THE FIELD...

EVERY PERSON WHO HAS EVER WORKED ON A TANK, FOR WHATEVER ARMY OR COUNTRY, KNOWS TOO WELL THAT THE HARDEST JOB IS TRACK AND SUSPENSION REPAIR. IT IS VERY SLOW, DIRTY, HEAVY, AND *DANGEROUS* WORK.

AND HOW ARE THE TYMOSHENKO SISTERS DOING, NOW THAT THEY ARE WEAPONLESS?

"WEAPONLESS," COMRADE CAPTAIN? WE SIMPLY WERE ISSUED SOMETHING A LITTLE *LARGER.*

CAPTAIN, I HAVE A QUESTION. IN KIEV, I USED TO LISTEN ON MY RADIO TO THE LENINGRAD PHILHARMONIC. ITS PIANIST WAS NAMED *NIKOLAY KOVCHENKO.*

I HEAR YOU ARE AND THE ONE AND THE SAME.

YES, THIS IS *TRUE.*

OH, THIS IS AN *HONOR!* I WAS WONDERING... IF THERE'S A PIANO AROUND HERE--

--PERHAPS YOU WOULD GRACE US WITH A SMALL CONCERT...?

STILL SMILING, THE CAPTAIN PULLED HIS LEFT HAND FROM HIS POCKET...

I'M AFRAID MY CONCERT DAYS ARE OVER.

CAPTAIN KOVCHENKO WALKED OFF WITH HIS CLIQUE...

...LEAVING ME FEELING TWO INCHES TALL.

HOW DO YOU *DO* IT, KATUSHA?

JUST RUN ME OVER WITH THE TANK, MILLA.

DO NOT BE *DISTRESSED,* COMRADE TYMOSHENKO...

...KOVCHENKO IS NOT THE SORT OF MAN TO BE OFFENDED.

CAPTAIN RAMSKOV'S WORDS WERE EXTREMELY WELCOME.

IT WAS IN THE COMMUNICATIONS AND RADIO CLASSES THAT I HAD A CHANCE TO REALLY SHINE...

WHEN *NORDRIN'S BRIGADE* IS REFORMED, EVERY TANK WILL AT LEAST HAVE A RADIO RECEIVER. THAT SHOULD MAKE A *BIG* DIFFERENCE.

IN SOVIET RUSSIA, RADIO TECHNOLOGY WAS STILL PRIMITIVE, DOUBLY SO FOR ITS TANK UNITS.

ANY ADVANTAGES THE *T-34S* HAD WERE WASTED WHEN GERMAN UNITS COULD EASILY OUTPERFORM THEM WITH BETTER COMMUNICATIONS.

WE STAYED SO BUSY THAT TIME SEEMED TO PASS MUCH TOO QUICKLY...

NIGHTS ARE GETTING MUCH *COLDER...!*

YES-- WINTER IS COMING.

I HOPE TARAS IS *WARM--AND SAFE...*

EVERY SOVIET CITIZEN WAS WATCHING THE EVENTS UNFOLDING IN *STALINGRAD*. WE KNEW THAT IF GERMANY WON, IT'D BE ALL OVER. WE UKRAINIANS WOULD HAVE TO DECIDE WHETHER WE WERE TO LIVE UNDER FASCIST DOMINATION--OR REMAIN EXILES FROM EVERYTHING WE HAD EVER KNOWN AND LOVED.

FROM WASHINGTON TO LONDON, THE EYES OF THE WORLD WERE ALSO FOCUSED ON THE CITY ON THE VOLGA...

IN THIS YEAR, *1942*, IT COULD ALL BE CHANGING--IN NORTH AFRICA, IN THE NORTH ATLANTIC, IN THE SOUTH PACIFIC...BUT IT ALL HINGED ON *STALINGRAD.* WINSTON CHURCHILL UNDERSTOOD THIS WHEN HE CALLED IT THE *"HINGE OF FATE."*

IN SEPTEMBER 1942, POLITICAL COMMANDER NIKITA KHRUSHCHEV TURNED OVER THE COMMAND OF THE *62ND ARMY* TO *GENERAL VASILY CHUIKOV.*

COMRADE CHUIKOV, HOW DO YOU INTERPRET YOUR TASK?

WE WILL *DEFEND* THE CITY--

--OR *DIE* IN THE ATTEMPT.

THE FIRST THING CHUIKOV DID WAS PLACE *NKVD* GUARDS AT EVERY DEPARTURE POINT ON THE WEST BANK OF THE RIVER. ANYONE ATTEMPTING TO CROSS THE VOLGA TO SAFETY, UNLESS CARRYING PROPER PERMISSION OR BADLY WOUNDED, WAS TO BE SUMMARILY *SHOT.*

THE *GERMAN 6TH ARMY,* TRAINED AND EXPERIENCED IN OPEN MECHANIZED WARFARE, WAS NOT PREPARED FOR THE CLOSE-IN, HAND-TO-HAND FIGHTING IN STALINGRAD.

CHUIKOV MADE IT CLEAR HOW THE BATTLE WAS TO BE FOUGHT. "EVERY GERMAN MUST BE MADE TO FEEL THAT HE IS LIVING UNDER THE MUZZLE OF A RUSSIAN GUN," HE TOLD HIS MEN.

BECAUSE OF THE FEROCITY OF THE FIGHTING, THE DEAD OF EITHER SIDE SELDOM WERE RECOVERED OR BURIED.

THE BODIES SEEMED TO COLLECT IN LAYERS ON THE GROUND, LIKE GEOLOGIC STRATA.

CHUIKOV TOLD HIS STAFF: "EVERY MAN MUST BECOME ONE OF THE STONES OF THE CITY."

MEN ON BOTH SIDES LIVED AND FOUGHT IN CELLARS AND SEWERS. FOOD WAS SCARCE. PEOPLE TURNED TO EATING HORSES, DOGS, CATS--EVEN RATS. MEN FOUGHT TO THE DEATH OVER ACCESS TO SOURCES OF MARGINALLY CLEAN WATER.

THE CITY DEVELOPED A SOCIETY AND CULTURE OF ITS OWN. A SONG AROSE THAT BECAME POPULAR AMONG THE ENTRENCHED AND EMBATTLED SOVIET TROOPS:

"ZEMLYANKA" OR "THE DUGOUT"-- ALSO KNOWN AS "THE FOUR STEPS TO DEATH."

IT WAS CONDEMNED BY THE AUTHORITIES BECAUSE OF ITS PESSIMISM--BUT THE COMMISSARS LEARNED TO LOOK THE OTHER WAY.

"THE FIRE IS FLICKERING IN THE NARROW STOVE... RESIN OOZES FROM THE LOG LIKE A TEAR, AND THE CONCERTINA IN THE BUNKER SINGS TO ME OF YOUR SMILE AND EYES..."

IN MOSCOW, STALIN WAS EXASPERATED WITH THE SITUATION.

NO! YOU ARE *ALL* BEING FAR TOO *SHORTSIGHTED!*

HOW CAN YOU NOT UNDERSTAND THAT IF WE *SURRENDER STALINGRAD*, THEN THE SOUTH OF THE COUNTRY WILL BE *CUT OFF* FROM THE CENTER--?!

THIS WILL BE NOT ONLY A *CATASTROPHE* FOR STALINGRAD ITSELF--!

DEPUTY SUPREME COMMANDER *GEORGY ZHUKOV*, THE MAN WHO'D ENGINEERED THE DEFENSE OF LENINGRAD AND MOSCOW, WAS NOT LOOKING ONLY AT STALINGRAD ON THE MAP...

HMM...

--BUT WE'LL LOSE OUR MAIN WATERWAY...AND SOON OUR OIL SOURCE, TOO!

ZHUKOV WAS SCRUTINIZING THE GERMANS' THINLY DEFENDED FLANKS, MANNED MAINLY BY ROMANIANS AND ITALIANS...

...YES.

RIGHT THERE...

...AND THERE...

AS OCTOBER 1942 DREW TO A CLOSE, WINTER WAS ALREADY DESCENDING UPON THE BATTLEFIELDS OF THIS SPRAWLING WAR. A STRONG, CHILL WIND HAD BEGUN TO BLOW...

...LIKE THE WINDS OF FATE THAT WERE BLOWING ON THE MADLY SWINGING DOOR OF HISTORY...

...AND ONLY THE *HINGE OF STALINGRAD* WOULD DETERMINE ON *WHOM* IT WOULD *SLAM SHUT.*

Katusha

OCTOBER 1942... THE GERMAN 6TH ARMY HAS CONQUERED MOST OF *STALINGRAD.* BUT SO LONG AS THE RUSSIANS HOLD ANY PART OF THE BANKS OF THE RIVER VOLGA, IT IS ALL FOR NOTHING. NOW THE GERMANS *MUST* TAKE THE FACTORY DISTRICT.

ONE IMPENETRABLE OBSTACLE STANDING IN THEIR WAY CAME IN THE FORM OF A FOUR-STORY BRICK APARTMENT BUILDING ON *SOLECHNAYA STREET* ON LENIN SQUARE.

THE BUILDING WAS HELD BY THREE DOZEN SOLDIERS UNDER THE COMMAND OF *SERGEANT JACOB PAVLOV,* WHO BECAME KNOWN AS *"THE HOUSEKEEPER."*

HIS MEN HAILED FROM NEARLY EVERY REPUBLIC IN THE *U.S.S.R.*: FROM KAZAKHSTAN, GEORGIA, UKRAINE, UZBEKISTAN...

SEVERAL *CIVILIANS* WHO WERE DISCOVERED HOLED UP IN THE BUILDING'S CELLAR ALSO TOOK AN *ACTIVE PART* IN THE DEFENSE.

SEARCHING THE BUILDING FOR USABLE ITEMS AND FOOD, A SOLDIER FOUND A WIND-UP *GRAMOPHONE* AND *ONE RECORD* WITH A PEELED-OFF LABEL...

DURING TIMES OF BOTH CALM AND MAYHEM, THEY PLAYED THE UNKNOWN TUNE...

IT PLAYED A TUNE NONE OF THEM RECOGNIZED.

THEY PLAYED IT UNTIL THE NEEDLE WORE THROUGH THE DISK.

DURING THE OCTOBER *PUTSCH*, THE GERMANS SENT FOUR TANKS AGAINST PAVLOV'S HOUSE. THEIR INTENTION WAS TO LEVEL THIS INFURIATING OBSTRUCTION.

PAVLOV SENT HIS MEN TO LOCATIONS IN THE BUILDING TO WHICH THE TANKS' GUNS COULD NOT ELEVATE.

YOU! FOURTH FLOOR!

THE *REST* OF YOU--DOWN IN THE *CELLAR!*

— HE THEN SENT OUT A COMBAT PATROL WITH A *14.5MM PTRD ANTI-TANK RIFLE.*

THE COMBAT PATROL SUCCEEDED SO THOROUGHLY IN KNOCKING OUT ONE OF THE TANKS THAT THE REST *WITHDREW.*

FOR *58 DAYS*, PAVLOV'S HOUSE HELD AGAINST THE GERMANS... DURING THAT TIME, AS *GENERAL CHUIKOV* LIKED TO POINT OUT, THEY KILLED MORE GERMANS THAN IT TOOK TO TAKE *PARIS.*

ON THE 62ND ARMY'S HEADQUARTERS MAP, CHUIKOV'S CODE NAME FOR PAVLOV'S HOUSE WAS *"THE LIGHTHOUSE."*

JACOB PAVLOV FOUGHT ON TO BERLIN, AND BECAME A *HERO* OF THE SOVIET UNION. BUT SOMEWHERE ALONG THAT BLOODY ROAD, HE MET *GOD...*

...AND HE SPENT THE REST OF HIS DAYS AS AN *ORTHODOX PRIEST.*

ON *OCTOBER 22*, THE FIRST SNOWS BEGAN TO FALL AT STALINGRAD.

ALREADY? ARE WE GOING TO HAVE TO GO THROUGH ANOTHER *RUSSIAN WINTER?*

OH, GOD, NO!

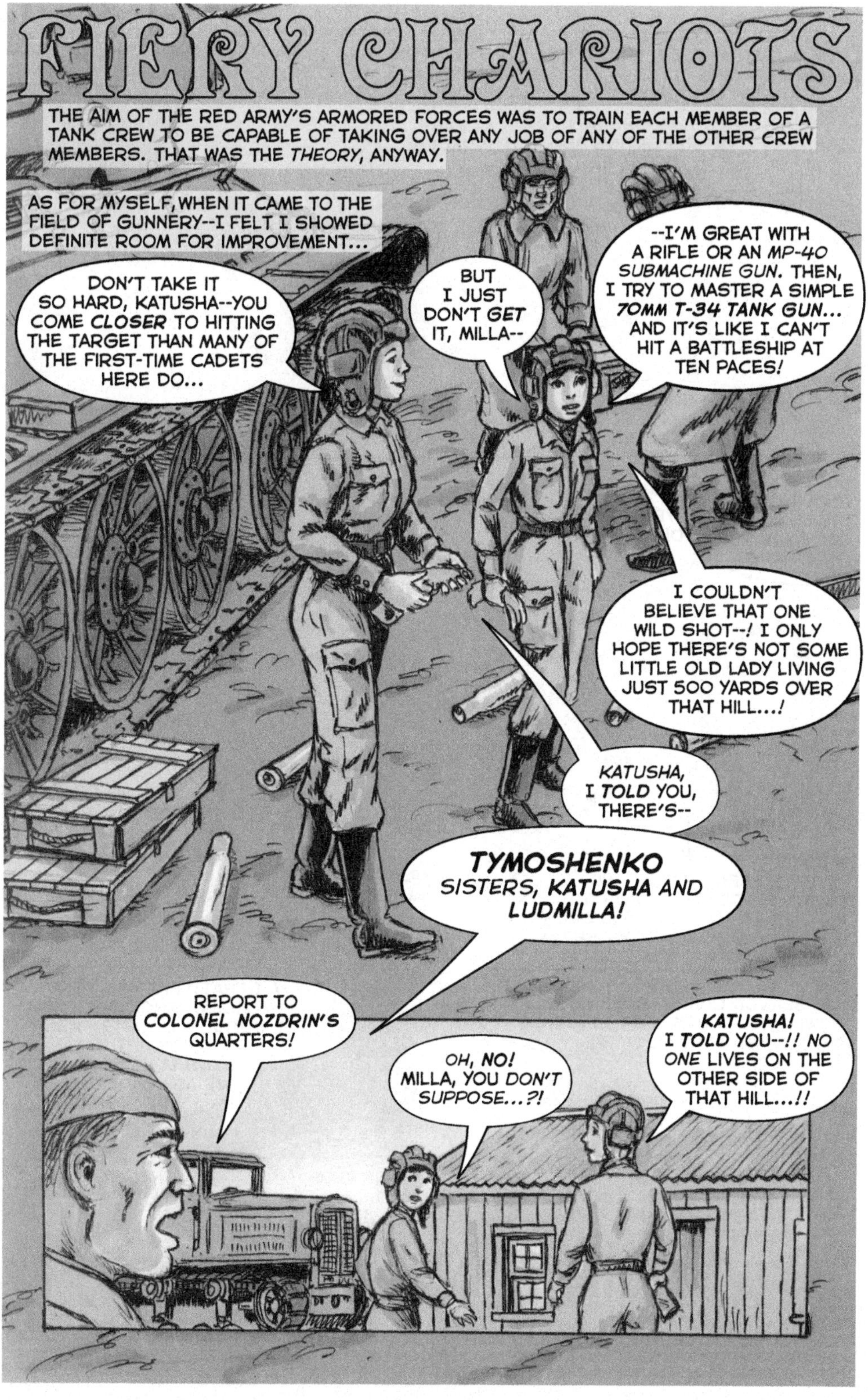
FIERY CHARIOTS
THE AIM OF THE RED ARMY'S ARMORED FORCES WAS TO TRAIN EACH MEMBER OF A TANK CREW TO BE CAPABLE OF TAKING OVER ANY JOB OF ANY OF THE OTHER CREW MEMBERS. THAT WAS THE *THEORY*, ANYWAY.
AS FOR MYSELF, WHEN IT CAME TO THE FIELD OF GUNNERY--I FELT I SHOWED DEFINITE ROOM FOR IMPROVEMENT...
DON'T TAKE IT SO HARD, KATUSHA--YOU COME ***CLOSER*** TO HITTING THE TARGET THAN MANY OF THE FIRST-TIME CADETS HERE DO...
BUT I JUST DON'T ***GET*** IT, MILLA--
--I'M GREAT WITH A RIFLE OR AN *MP-40 SUBMACHINE GUN*. THEN, I TRY TO MASTER A SIMPLE ***70MM T-34 TANK GUN...*** AND IT'S LIKE I CAN'T HIT A BATTLESHIP AT TEN PACES!
I COULDN'T BELIEVE THAT ONE WILD SHOT--! I ONLY HOPE THERE'S NOT SOME LITTLE OLD LADY LIVING JUST 500 YARDS OVER THAT HILL...!
*KATUSHA, I **TOLD** YOU, THERE'S--*
TYMOSHENKO *SISTERS*, **KATUSHA** *AND* **LUDMILLA!**
REPORT TO **COLONEL NOZDRIN'S** QUARTERS!
OH, ***NO!*** *MILLA, YOU* ***DON'T*** *SUPPOSE...?!*
KATUSHA! *I* ***TOLD*** *YOU--!! NO* ***ONE*** *LIVES ON THE OTHER SIDE OF THAT HILL...!!*

LIEUTENANT COLONEL RUSLAN NOZDRIN HAD DISTINGUISHED HIMSELF IN THE DEFENSE OF MOSCOW--BUT IN THE PROCESS, MOST OF HIS TANK BRIGADE HAD BEEN WIPED OUT. WE WERE TRAINING TO BE PART OF HIS NEW BRIGADE. WE FOUND COLONEL NOZDRIN WORKING AT HIS CLUTTERED DESK...CLUTTER BEING FURTHER JUMBLED BY AN ORANGE KITTEN.

TYMOSHENKO, REPORTING AS ORDERED!

AT EASE, COMRADES...

I UNDERSTAND THAT YOU HAVE BOTH SEEN COMBAT BEFORE...UNDER WHOSE COMMAND WAS THAT?

UNDER OUR UNCLE TARAS, SIR. WE WERE PARTISANS.

YES, IN A DIFFERENT KIND OF WAR.

FROM WHAT I HAVE HEARD--

--YOU'VE BEEN SHOT AT AND DRAWN BLOOD. THAT IS WHAT'S IMPORTANT. KATUSHA, YOU SHOW STRONG COMMUNICATIONS SKILLS.

AND MILLA, YOU WERE SINGLED OUT AS BEING A VERY GOOD DRIVER.

CONSEQUENTLY... I HAVE CHOSEN YOU TO CREW MY COMMAND TANK AS DRIVER AND RADIO OPERATOR.

THIS IS SENIOR SERGEANT MISHA BOVA. HE SERVED OUR BRIGADE WELL LAST WINTER. HE HAS JUST RETURNED FROM THE HOSPITAL.

HE WILL BE OUR GUNNER.

IN BATTLE, I WILL SERVE AS LOADER. SINCE MY COMMAND DUTIES WILL OFTEN KEEP ME AWAY FROM THE TANK-- KATUSHA WILL FILL IN FOR ME AS LOADER WHEN NECESSARY.

MILLA AND I WERE *WALKING ON AIR...!*

HOW IN THE WORLD DID WE MANAGE TO DO *THAT?*

SOMEONE HIGH UP LIKES US--AT LEAST THEY DON'T THINK OF US AS *"DUMB TUFTIES."*

UH-OH! *OFFICERS* COMING--!

IT WAS CAPTAINS KOVCHENKO AND RAMSKOV. IT SEEMED THEY WERE ALREADY AWARE OF OUR APPOINTMENT.

I'VE ONLY A MOMENT, BUT I WANTED TO OFFER MY HEARTY *CONGRATULATIONS* TO BOTH OF YOU!

THANK YOU, COMRADE *CAPTAIN!*

AND I, TOO, WISH YOU *WELL.*

THANK YOU ALSO, CAPTAIN RAMSKOV. *UH,* SIR...? I KNOW CAPTAIN KOVCHENKO IS AN INSTRUCTOR HERE AT THE SCHOOL, BUT WHAT CLASS DOES HE TEACH?

RAMSKOV'S DISFIGURED FACE DID NOT CHANGE-- BUT I SWEAR I ALMOST SAW THE TWINKLING OF A *SMILE* IN HIS ONE EYE...

CAPTAIN KOVCHENKO COMMANDS THE *INFANTRY BATTALION*--THE ONE THAT WILL RIDE YOUR BRIGADE'S TANKS INTO BATTLE.

HMM, WHAT DO YOU THINK OF THAT? I HEAR INFANTRY OFFICERS LIKE TO RIDE A TANK'S BOW MACHINE GUN...

YEAH, SO--?

THAT MEANS KOVCHENKO'S *BUTT* WILL BE SITTING JUST *INCHES* ABOVE YOUR HEAD!

MILLA?! JUST *SHUT* UP...!

WHEN WE WALKED BACK INTO THE BARRACKS, WE COULD JUDGE FROM THE FROSTY RECEPTION THAT THEY'D ALREADY GOT THE WORD, TOO.

MARUSYA POZHARSKY HAD GOOD WISHES TO GIVE US--BUT SHE WAS THE ONLY ONE OF OUR BUNKMATES WHO DID.

THAT'S *GREAT* NEWS!

THANKS, MARUSYA. WE WERE JUST *LUCKY*--

HA! "*LUCK*"?! 'S *THAT* WHAT THEY CALL IT BACK WHERE YER FROM, YA LITTLE TUFTY *GINCH*?!!

OXANNA PEREPELITSYN--! I *KNEW* IT...! THAT GIRL HAD A REPUTATION FOR BEING AS TOUGH AS THE *DEVIL.*

WE'RE *NOT* IDIOTS! ALL OF US KNOW DAMN WELL JUST *HOW* YOU BACK-COUNTRY SLUTS PAID OFF "OLD BULLET HEAD" FOR STINKIN' *PRIVILEGES*--

OXANNA HAD OBVIOUSLY BEEN BORN WITH A BAD HARELIP, *AND* A CHIP ON HER SHOULDER...

--WITH A NICE, FAT PIECE OF YOUR CUTE LITTLE "*LUCK*"!

I REALLY FELT SORRY FOR HER--EVEN THOUGH SHE WANTED TO WHIP MY BUTT.

OXANNA, THE ONLY THING I GIVE COLONEL NOZDRIN IS THE THE RESPECT DUE HIS RANK...

I'M SURE THAT YOU COULD DO JUST AS WELL AS I...

DON'T GIMME THAT *CRAP!* YOU WALTZ IN HERE *LATE,* RIGHT OFFA THE *FARM,* AN' GET *PROMOTED,* BEFORE THE *REST* OF US--?!

WELL, YER *NOT* GONNA "*LUCK*" YER WAY OUTTA *PAYING* FOR IT *HERE AND NOW*--!!

MILLA WAS ABOUT TO JUMP INTO THE SITUATION, UNTIL I SHOT HER A WARNING GLANCE. SHE STOOD DOWN--BUT I KNEW SHE HAD MY BACK.

THEN, VERY CALMLY, I TURNED BACK TO OXANNA...

OXANNA--NO MATTER *WHAT* I SAY, YOU'RE JUST GONNA GO OFF...

...SO *WHY* DON'T YOU *SHUT UP,* AND GET TO IT?!

OXANNA *CHARGED ME* LIKE AN ANGRY BULL.

I'M A SMALL TARGET, SO I JUST SIDE-STEPPED HER.

I HAD ANOTHER ADVANTAGE. SHE WAS *BAREFOOT*...

...AND I WAS STILL WEARING MY *BOOTS.*

I KNEW THAT'D BE JUST ENOUGH TO GET HER REALLY *MAD...!* SO AS SHE PASSED ME--

--I DROVE MY SKINNY LITTLE ELBOW INTO HER LOWER BACK!

AND THEN OXANNA *HIT THE FLOOR* LIKE A SACK OF BAD BEETS!

WHY, KATUSHA! TARAS WOULD BE *PROUD* OF YOU!

BUT OXANNA WASN'T DOWN FOR LONG...!

BECAUSE OF HER DISTORTED FEATURES, I REALLY *DIDN'T* WANT TO HIT OXANNA IN HER FACE...

...BUT I WASN'T GOING TO LET MY SENSE OF GOOD SPORTSMANSHIP--

--KEEP ME FROM *PROTECTING* MYSELF.

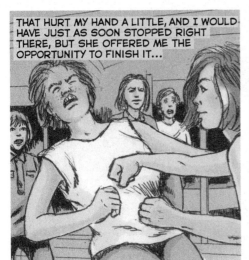

THAT HURT MY HAND A LITTLE, AND I WOULD HAVE JUST AS SOON STOPPED RIGHT THERE, BUT SHE OFFERED ME THE OPPORTUNITY TO FINISH IT...

...RIGHT IN THE **SOLAR PLEXUS!**

OXANNA FELL BACK ON A BUNK AND THEN BOUNCED ONTO THE FLOOR, HER EYES WIDE AND HER BREATH SHALLOW.

SOME OF HER ROUGH FRIENDS PICKED HER UP AND CARRIED HER TO HER BUNK, ALL OF THEM GIVING ME HARD GLARES.

HEY, **I** DIDN'T START THIS WHOLE THING. BUT I HOLD **NO GRUDGES.**

GETTING READY FOR BED THAT NIGHT, EVERYONE GAVE ME **WIDE BERTH.**

WHAT IS IT ABOUT LIFE, WHERE A GOOD THING HAPPENS--THEN SOMETHING BAD ALWAYS COMES ALONG THAT KEEPS YOU FROM ENJOYING IT? I REMEMBER WHEN I WAS YOUNG THINKING THAT I SURELY WOULDN'T HAVE THESE BAD FEELINGS WHEN I GOT OLDER. DO I HAVE TO GROW OLDER STILL? DO I HAVE TO GROW ALL THE WAY UP?

WHAT IS MATURITY?

WHAT DOES BEING "MATURE" REALLY MEAN? DO WE EVER REACH FULL MATURITY? WILL I KNOW WHEN IT COMES?

I WAS SUDDENLY AFRAID WITH THE COMING OF MATURITY, I WOULD BE LOSING THE JOYS OF YOUTH. I DIDN'T WANT TO DO THAT...NOT *YET*...

39

SEVERAL DAYS LATER--ON *NOVEMBER 3RD,* IF I CAN REMEMBER CORRECTLY-- A MESSENGER CAME TO CAPTAIN RAMSKOV'S CLASS BEARING AN IMPORTANT NOTE.

STUDENTS... TRAINING HAS *ENDED.*

CREW ASSIGNMENTS ARE LISTED ON THE BOARD OUTSIDE EACH BARRACKS. BE PACKED AND READY TO MOVE OUT IN *6 HOURS.*

WHA--?!

CAPTAIN RAMSKOV STOPPED US AS WE LEFT THE ROOM.

COLONEL NOZDRIN PASSED ON A MESSAGE FROM YOUR *FATHER...*

"*I WILL LOOK FOR YOU AT THE FACTORY.*"

THAT REALLY GOT OUR BLOOD FLOWING!

MISHA BOVA WAS WAITING FOR US WHEN WE CAME OUT.

SO--ARE THE TYMOSHENKO SISTERS ALL READY TO GO TO *WAR?*

WHAT-- *AGAIN?*

OH, HOW I *WISH* I'D BEEN KIDDING...

EVERYONE WAS ISSUED A PAIR OF FELT *VALENKI* BOOTS AND A BRAND-NEW SHEEPSKIN COAT.

EACH OF THE COMMANDERS WAS GIVEN A WRISTWATCH AND A FOUNTAIN PEN--AND SINCE WE WERE BOTH CREW MEMBERS OF THE BRIGADE COMMANDER'S TANK, MILLA AND I ALSO RECEIVED THEM.

MY FIRST WATCH!

WE WERE EACH ISSUED A SILK HANDKERCHIEF.

DON'T BLOW YOUR NOSE ON THAT!

IT'S FOR *FILTERING FUEL.*

40

TRUE TO THEIR WORD, TRUCKS WERE WAITING AND READY FOR US IN SIX HOURS...

MOST BRIGADES UP TO THAT TIME WERE A FIFTY-FIFTY MIX OF *T-34*s AND LIGHT TANKS LIKE THE LITTLE *T-70*s. BUT NOT US! WE WERE TO HAVE *THREE FULL BATTALIONS* OF *T-34*s--THAT'S *64 MEDIUM TANKS!* THAT IS A LOT OF POWER.

WE BOARDED THE TRUCKS AND HEADED IN THREE DIRECTIONS TO PICK UP OUR *T-34*s; THE *2ND BATTALION* TO THE *CHELYABINSK TRACTOR PLANT*, THE *3RD BATTALION* TO THE *SVERDLOVSK HEAVY MACHINERY FACTORY*, AND THE *1ST BATTALION*--AND OUR GROUP, THE *HEADQUARTERS SECTION*--WOULD HEAD TO THE *NIZHNIY TAGIL URAL CAR PLANT*.

THE TRUCK RIDE WAS LONG, ROUGH, AND BUMPY. WE WERE ALL TOO KEYED UP TO SLEEP.

BESIDES, THE VETERAN TANKERS KEPT US WIDE-EYED WITH HAIR-RAISING STORIES OF BLOODY BATTLES--ALL DESIGNED TO GIVE THE NEW TRAINEES *NIGHTMARES*.

IT WAS WELL AFTER DARK WHEN WE REACHED *NIZHNIY TAGIL*, BUT THAT DIDN'T MATTER BECAUSE THE HUGE FACTORY LIT UP THE NIGHT. IT BUZZED, CRACKLED, WHIRRED, AND SCREECHED WITH CONSTANT ACTIVITY.

IT WAS HARD TO BELIEVE THAT JUST A YEAR AGO, THIS HAD BEEN PEACEFUL FARMLAND.

THE *INSIDE* OF THE FACTORY WAS EVEN *MORE DRAMATIC.* IN AN INDUSTRIAL BALLET OF FLESH AND METAL, THE WORKERS--OLD MEN, WOMEN, AND EVEN CHILDREN--HANDLED THIS HEAVY EQUIPMENT WITH THE EASE OF ME PICKING BERRIES AT HOME. BUT THEIR SEEMING EASE WAS DECEPTIVE, FOR THEIR LABOR WAS ON A MONUMENTAL SCALE. IN A CEASELESS, CLANGING DANCE, THESE PLAIN, COMMON FOLKS WERE TURNING OUT TANK AFTER TANK AFTER *TANK* AFTER *TANK...!*

...AND *T-34S,* NO LESS.

THEY ASSIGNED US TO POSITIONS ON THE ASSEMBLY LINES, IDEALLY IN OUR AREAS OF EXPERTISE. THE GIRL WHO SHOWED ME HOW TO INSTALL THE 9R RADIO COULDN'T HAVE BEEN OVER FOURTEEN...!

MILLA WORKED WITH A FRAIL OLD MAN MOUNTING THE DRIVER'S ELECTRONIC DEVICES AND GAUGES.

NO ONE WATCHED THE CLOCK. WE KEPT AT IT, TIRED, COLD, AND HUNGRY... BUT NOT A SOUL COMPLAINED. THESE WERE THE SLEDS THAT WOULD CONVEY US TO WAR-- OUR *"FIERY CHARIOTS."*

WE WANTED THESE TANKS TO BE *PERFECT.* AND NONE OF US WANTED THE FACTORY WORKERS TO THINK THAT OUR STANDARDS WERE ANY LESS EXACTING THAN *THEIRS.*

FOR A CHANGE, PAPA FOUND *ME* BUSY WORKING ON MACHINERY. I COULD TELL HE WAS PROUD OF US. IT WAS WONDERFUL TO SEE HIS SMILE, ESPECIALLY AFTER HAVING TO LEAVE HIM BEHIND IN STALINGRAD.

AH! HERE COMES HALF OF MY *TEAM!* LET'S FIND MILLA--

--I HAVE SOMETHING TO SHOW YOU.

WELL, THERE SHE *IS*--! JUST AS *PERFECT* AS WE CAN MAKE THEM...

AND HOPEFULLY, SHE'LL PROVE HERSELF WORTHY ENOUGH TO TAKE MY GIRLS INTO *HARM'S WAY*--

--AND BRING THEM *BACK OUT* OF IT *SAFELY!*

WOW!

PAPA SURE HAD A KNACK FOR PICKING OUT *BIG PRESENTS!* FIRST, HE GAVE ME *MILLA*-- AND NOW, OUR VERY OWN *T-34* TANK!

I LAUGHED AND REACHED OUT TO STROKE MY NEW TOY--BUT AS I RAN MY HAND OVER THE ARMOR PLATING...

...THE FEEL OF THE COLD, HARD METAL AGAINST MY FINGERTIPS BEGAN TO GIVE ME THE *STRANGEST SENSATION...!*

YES, THIS TANK *WAS* A *SHE*--BUT WITH NO HEART, NO BRAIN, NO SOUL...! AND PERHAPS THAT WAS AS IT *SHOULD* BE.

I KNEW IN THAT INSTANT THIS MACHINE WOULD BE THE KIND OF IMPLEMENT THAT WOULD ALLOW US TO DO WHAT WE HAD TO DO--BECAUSE...

...SHE WAS A REAL *BITCH!*

WE EACH GAVE PAPA ONE LAST HUG AND KISS, THEN TURNED TO GO...

SOVIET TANK CREWS HOLD THE RANK OF JUNIOR SERGEANT OR ABOVE, SO UPON THE RECEIPT OF OUR TANK, MILLA AND I GOT AUTOMATICALLY *PROMOTED...!*

SO WE CLIMBED ABOARD OUR *T-34* AS *JUNIOR SERGEANTS.*

THE DIESEL ENGINE ROLLED OVER AND ROARED AT MILLA'S FIRST TRY.

T-34S ARE VERY LOUD-- BUT THAT WAS ALL RIGHT. WE WEREN'T PLANNING ON SNEAKING UP ON ANYONE.

THE TRACKS CLANKED ESPECIALLY LOUDLY, SINCE AT THAT TIME THERE WAS A SHORTAGE OF RUBBER. FEW ROAD WHEELS HAD RUBBER RIMS.

MILLA GUIDED US SMOOTHLY THROUGH THE BIG ROLL-UP DOORS. I TUNED THE RADIO IN CLEARLY, AND I HEARD COLONEL NOZDRIN AS HE DIRECTED US UP TO THE HEAD OF THE COLUMN.

HE WOULD BE THERE, IN HIS *GAZ67-B* FIELD CAR WITH HIS DRIVER, VERA FYODOROVICH.

WITH THE COLONEL OUT IN FRONT, AND US RIGHT BEHIND HIM...

...WE LED THE COLUMN DOWN A LONG, STRAIGHT, GRAVELLED ROAD.

44

WE HAD NOT SLEPT SINCE WE LEFT THE SCHOOL AT CHELYABINSK, BUT WE WERE STILL TOO KEYED UP TO BE BOTHERED. BACK THEN IN OUR YOUTH, WE WERE ABLE TO GO FOR MANY, MANY HOURS BEFORE FATIGUE FINALLY CAUGHT UP WITH US...

STILL, IT WAS COLD IN THE TANK-- AND THE ENGINE FANS IN THE REAR OF THE CREW COMPARTMENT PULLED IN A BRISK DRAFT OF ICY AIR THROUGH THE DRIVER'S HATCH.

OUR HEADLIGHTS GLEAMING, WE CONTINUED TO MOVE THROUGH HEAVY WOODS, KNOWING THAT THE NEAREST GERMAN PLANE WAS MANY HUNDREDS OF MILES AWAY.

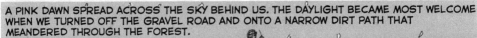

A PINK DAWN SPREAD ACROSS THE SKY BEHIND US. THE DAYLIGHT BECAME MOST WELCOME WHEN WE TURNED OFF THE GRAVEL ROAD AND ONTO A NARROW DIRT PATH THAT MEANDERED THROUGH THE FOREST.

SINCE WE WERE AT THE HEAD OF THE COLUMN, THE DIRT SURFACE WAS FINE. BUT--THE MORE OF US THAT PASSED, THE MORE CHURNED UP IT BECAME.

A FEW TANKS TOWARD THE REAR OF THE COLUMN BEGAN TO BOG DOWN AND GET STUCK.

LUCKILY, THE VETERAN TANKERS KNEW HOW TO EXTRACT THEIR *T-34*S FROM THE MUD BY CUTTING DOWN SMALL TREES AND JAMMING THE LOGS UNDER THE TRACKS.

SINCE OUR PACE WAS NEVER MORE THAN 15 MPH, THOSE TANKS THAT SUFFERED THIS DELAY WERE ABLE TO KEEP UP.

45

THE SUN WAS DOWN BEYOND THE TREES WHEN WE REACHED A LARGE STUBBLED WHEAT FIELD NEAR A SMALL VILLAGE NEAR A LITTLE RIVER. THE TRUCKS OF OUR MAINTENANCE AND SUPPLY COMPANIES WERE ALREADY THERE, BUT OUR TWO OTHER TANK BATTALIONS HAD NOT YET ARRIVED.

PARK THEM ACCORDING TO PLATOON AND COMPANY, AND GET THE MAINTENANCE REPORTS COMPLETED.

THEN WE CAN POST SENTRIES AND LET EVERYONE TURN IN.

EACH TANK HAD A MAINTENANCE LOG, AND NONE OF ITS CREW COULD SLEEP UNTIL ALL PROCEDURES HAD BEEN FOLLOWED AND THE TANK DECLARED READY TO FIGHT AT DAWN.

THIS MIGHT BE A GOOD TIME FOR A LITTLE EXPLANATION.

SO FAR, YOU'VE SEEN A LOT OF WOMEN SOLDIERS AT THE CHELYABINSK TANK SCHOOL AND OTHER PLACES. BUT OUR BRIGADE NEVER WAS MORE THAN SIX PERCENT FEMALE. IN OUR TANKS, THERE WERE AROUND A DOZEN DRIVERS AND ASSISTANT DRIVERS.

LATER IN THE WAR, THERE WOULD BE SOME UNITS MADE UP ALMOST ENTIRELY OF GIRLS JUST LIKE ME.

A FEW WOMEN MANNED ANTI-TANK AND ANTI-AIRCRAFT BATTERIES, AND SEVERAL SERVED IN THE HEADQUARTERS STAFF.

BUT THE MEDICAL SECTION, INCLUDING DOCTORS, WAS PREDOMINANTLY FEMALE. YOUNG GIRL MEDICS WOULD DART OUT ONTO THE BATTLEFIELD UNDER FIRE TO DRAG WOUNDED SOLDIERS, OFTEN TWICE THEIR SIZE, TO AN AID STATION...

THESE VALIANT WOMEN WERE HELD IN UNIVERSAL RESPECT!

WE DID OUR MAINTENANCE, BUILT FIRES, AND HAD A SIMPLE BUT TASTY MEAL OF BREAD AND HORSE SAUSAGE THAT WE HAD RECEIVED BACK IN CHELYABINSK.

DO YOU LIKE HORSE SAUSAGE?

AS LONG AS I DIDN'T *KNOW* THE HORSE...!

THEN WE CURLED UP IN THE TARPAULIN THAT EVERY TANK CARRIED AND WENT TO SLEEP.

LATER IN THE NIGHT, I WAS AWAKENED BY A STRANGE SENSATION--THE EARTH WAS *SHAKING!*

--AAH...?!!

IS THIS WHAT AN *EARTHQUAKE* IS LIKE?, I THOUGHT FOR A MOMENT...

THEN I REALIZED THAT THE VIBRATIONS WERE MERELY THE SOUNDS OF OUR 2ND AND 3RD BATTALIONS ARRIVING AT OUR MEETUP POINT.

THE SOUND OF FORTY-TWO *T-34*S RUMBLING ACROSS THE EARTH AT ONCE WILL SHAKE YOU TO THE CORE. RECALLING IT REMINDS ME OF A LINE FROM A POEM I WAS TO HEAR LATER IN THE WAR...

"A WAR ISN'T FIREWORKS AT ALL-- JUST HEAVY DAILY LABOR..."

AND THE VETERAN TANKERS...?

⋛GZZZKH⋚

THEY SLEPT THROUGH THIS TUMULTUOUS ARRIVAL AS IF IT WERE NOTHING MORE THAN THE RISING OF THE MOON.

EARLY NEXT MORNING, THE WHOLE BRIGADE WAS UP AND READY FOR FIRING PRACTICE WITH THE NEW TANKS.

WE'VE GOT LOCAL CARPENTERS BUILDING TARGETS FROM OLD SLEDS AND WAGONS...

I WANT THE NEW MEN TO GO IN FIRST-- AND THEN THE VETERANS TO SHOW HOW IT'S REALLY DONE.

ON THE WAY TO OUR RANGE, I SAW SOME OF THE GUNNERY INSTRUCTORS FROM THE SCHOOL, AND TO OUR SURPRISE...

CAPTAIN RAMSKOV!

HELLO!

HIS POOR, BROKEN FACE COULD NOT SMILE, BUT HE GAVE ME A CRISP SALUTE.

THE NEW GUNNERS DID NOT DO BADLY AT ALL, PERFORMING THEIR DUTIES JUST AS THEY'D BEEN TAUGHT--

--"BY THE BOOK," AS THEY SAY.

THEN THE VETERANS TOOK OVER, AND WE WERE MOST IMPRESSED...!

I GUESS JUST THE FACT THAT THEY HAD SURVIVED THE FIRST YEAR OF THIS WAR REALLY SAYS IT ALL...

BUT THE REAL SURPRISE WAS OUR OWN GUNNER, MISHA BOVA. TIME AFTER TIME, HE HIT THE TARGET WHILE OUR TANK WAS MOVING--AND THE TARGET WAS BEING PULLED!

IF THE DRIVER CAN KEEP ME INFORMED ABOUT THE LAND AHEAD, AND THE TARGET IS LYING WITHIN ELEVEN O'CLOCK AND ONE O'CLOCK--

--I CAN HIT IT *EVERY* TIME!

I LOADED FOR MISHA DURING THE EXERCISE, AND THIS IS WHAT I DIDN'T LIKE ABOUT IT: THE FUMES FROM THE GUN CAN MAKE YOU PASS OUT. IT'S ALL RIGHT IF THE LOADER'S HATCH IS OPEN...

OTHERWISE, AFTER THREE OR FOUR SHOTS, YOU'LL BE ON THE FLOOR.

THREE DAYS LATER, WE WERE ON THE MOVE AGAIN-- THIS TIME TO A RAILHEAD 25 MILES AWAY.

ONCE THERE, WE FUELED OUR TANKS TO THE BRIM, THEN LOADED OUR STEEDS ON FLATCARS.

49

SO...IS THIS AS FAR AS YOU GO WITH US, CAPTAIN RAMSKOV?

YES, COMRADE TYMOSHENKO--THIS IS IT. I MUST NOW BE HEADING BACK TO CHELYABINSK.

CAPTAIN, I WISH TO THANK YOU FOR ALL THAT YOU'VE DONE FOR US...

I SHOWED MY APPRECIATION IN THE ONLY WAY THAT FELT APPROPRIATE...

--?!

YOU TAUGHT ME WELL, CAPTAIN--AND I PROMISE THAT I WILL MAKE YOU PROUD.

I KNOW YOU SHALL.

FAREWELL, COMRADE.

ON THIS TRIP, SOME OF THE NEWNESS AND WONDER HAD FINALLY BEGUN TO WEAR OFF...

...AND I SLEPT LIKE A BABY.

50

WE RODE THE TRAIN FOR FOUR DAYS. IT WAS GOOD WE HAD THE OPPORTUNITY TO REST ON THE TRIP, BECAUSE THE NEXT SEVERAL DAYS WOULD BE VERY HECTIC.

AT LEAST A DOZEN MORE TRAINS WERE FOLLOWING OURS, CARRYING THE REST OF OUR BRIGADE.

WE DISEMBARKED NEAR A LITTLE TOWN BESIDE A RIVER, WHICH TURNED OUT TO BE THE *DON*. THE FIRST THING I NOTICED WAS THE DOZENS OF LARGE FERRY BOATS AWAITING US.

DAY AND NIGHT, THEY FERRIED US ACROSS THE RIVER. IT TOOK TWO AND A HALF DAYS, AND THERE WERE NO MISHAPS OR ACCIDENTS. FORTUNATELY, THE WEATHER HAD TURNED BAD--CLOUDY SKIES AND THE STEADY SNOWFALL WOULD HELP COVER OUR MOVEMENTS IN CASE A GERMAN PLANE FLEW OVER.

AFTER WE GOT ACROSS, WE THEN MOVED OUR TANKS IN AND AROUND SEVERAL VILLAGES IN THE AREA.

A TRUCK CAME AROUND WITH BUCKETS OF WHITEWASH TO CAMOUFLAGE OUR TANKS.

MORE TRUCKS BROUGHT IN HAY. WE USED IT TO COVER OUR VEHICLES TO MAKE THEM LOOK LIKE HOUSES AND BARNS...

...AND WE ALLOWED THE POOR SKINNY LOCAL FARM ANIMALS TO EAT THEIR FILL.

LATER THAT DAY, OUR INFANTRY BATTALION MARCHED IN, ALL DECKED OUT IN NEW WHITE SNOW SUITS...

I JUST GOT WORD FROM HEADQUARTERS-- TOMORROW, THERE'LL BE A PERFORMANCE BY A MUSICAL TROUPE!

WOW! WHEN?

NOON, IN THE NEXT VILLAGE!

52

THE CONCERT WAS HELD IN A LITTLE BOWL-SHAPED AREA NEAR THE RIVER. THE ENTIRE BRIGADE--TANKERS, INFANTRY, AND SERVICE PEOPLE--COVERED THE SIDES OF THE BOWL. THE "STAGE" WAS A HAY-COVERED FLAT AT THE BOTTOM, WITH AN OLD BEAT-UP UPRIGHT PIANO AND ONE OF OUR TANKS FOR A BACKDROP. THE PERFORMERS WERE VERY GOOD. SIX GIRLS SANG, ACCOMPANIED BY THREE GUYS ON A BALALAIKA, AN ACCORDION, AND THAT PIANO, PLAYING POPULAR AND PATRIOTIC SONGS...

SUDDENLY, *CAPTAIN KOVCHENKO* STEPPED OUT IN FRONT OF THE CROWD...

...AND THE INFANTRY SOLDIERS WENT *WILD!*

NOT LONG AGO, SOMEONE ASKED ME IF I WOULD PERFORM A CONCERT. I REPLIED THEN THAT MY CONCERT DAYS WERE OVER...

BUT IN THIS COMPANY, I THOUGHT I MIGHT AS WELL GIVE IT A *TRY...*

THE CROWD ROARED ITS APPROVAL--AND THEN FELL UTTERLY *SILENT.*

HE BEGAN WITH "DARK EYES" THEN "MOSCOW NIGHTS"... DESPITE HIS DAMAGED HAND AND THE BEAT-UP PIANO, THE BEAUTIFUL STRAINS OF HIS MUSIC FLOWED UP AROUND US.

THE HUSHED AUDIENCE SWAYED ALONG IN TIME.

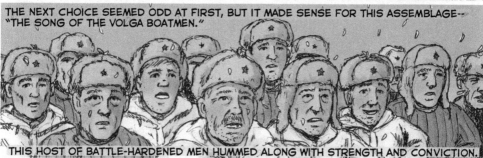

THE NEXT CHOICE SEEMED ODD AT FIRST, BUT IT MADE SENSE FOR THIS ASSEMBLAGE-- "THE SONG OF THE VOLGA BOATMEN."

THIS HOST OF BATTLE-HARDENED MEN HUMMED ALONG WITH STRENGTH AND CONVICTION.

I OVERHEARD THE TWO GIRLS BY US WHISPERING...

...HE'S ONLY TWENTY-SIX YEARS OLD...

...CHILD PRODIGY AT THE LENINGRAD CONSERVATORY...

...DIMITRY SHOSTAKOVICH IS HIS GOOD FRIEND...

...HIS WIFE IS A TALENTED VIOLINIST...

:AAH!:

THEIR LAST COMMENT HIT ME DEEP IN MY STOMACH.

KOVCHENKO ENDED HIS CONCERT WITH "MY COUNTRY." THE BRIGADE ROSE TO ITS FEET AND RESPONDED IN SONG. BUT AS I ROSE, I REFLECTED IN MY HEART...

THIS IS NOT *MY* COUNTRY. WHAT AM I DOING HERE?

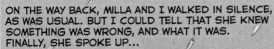

ON THE WAY BACK, MILLA AND I WALKED IN SILENCE, AS WAS USUAL. BUT I COULD TELL THAT SHE KNEW SOMETHING WAS WRONG, AND WHAT IT WAS. FINALLY, SHE SPOKE UP...

YOU KNOW, KATUSHA...HE IS *RUSSIAN*.

AND WE WANT TO GO HOME TO *UKRAINE*.

YEAH...

THAT'S RIGHT...

I FELT MY FROSTY SILENCE THAWING...

...THEN IT ALL *BURST OUT*.

HOW DID WE EVEN GET HERE, MILLA? THE PATH THAT WE'VE TAKEN IS BEYOND BELIEF--!

--AND WHY IN THE WORLD IS *HE* THE ONE WHO MOVES ME?

DEAR, DEAR KATUSHA... YOU ARE *NOT* RESPONSIBLE FOR THE DIRECTION YOUR HEART PULLS YOU...

...YOU ARE ONLY RESPONSIBLE IF YOU *FOLLOW* IT.

THESE THINGS THAT I AM TELLING YOU SEEM SO INSIGNIFICANT-- EVEN SILLY. BUT THEY WERE NOT--THEY WOULD HAVE AN EFFECT ON MY WHOLE LIFE.

ASK YOURSELF--WHO CANNOT REMEMBER WHEN THEY FIRST FELL IN LOVE? EVERY ONE OF US CAN.

BUT--WHO CAN REMEMBER GREAT EARTHSHAKING EVENTS, LIKE THE *BATTLE OF STALINGRAD?*

I CAN REMEMBER THEM BOTH...

I CAN REMEMBER THEM BECAUSE I WAS *THERE*.

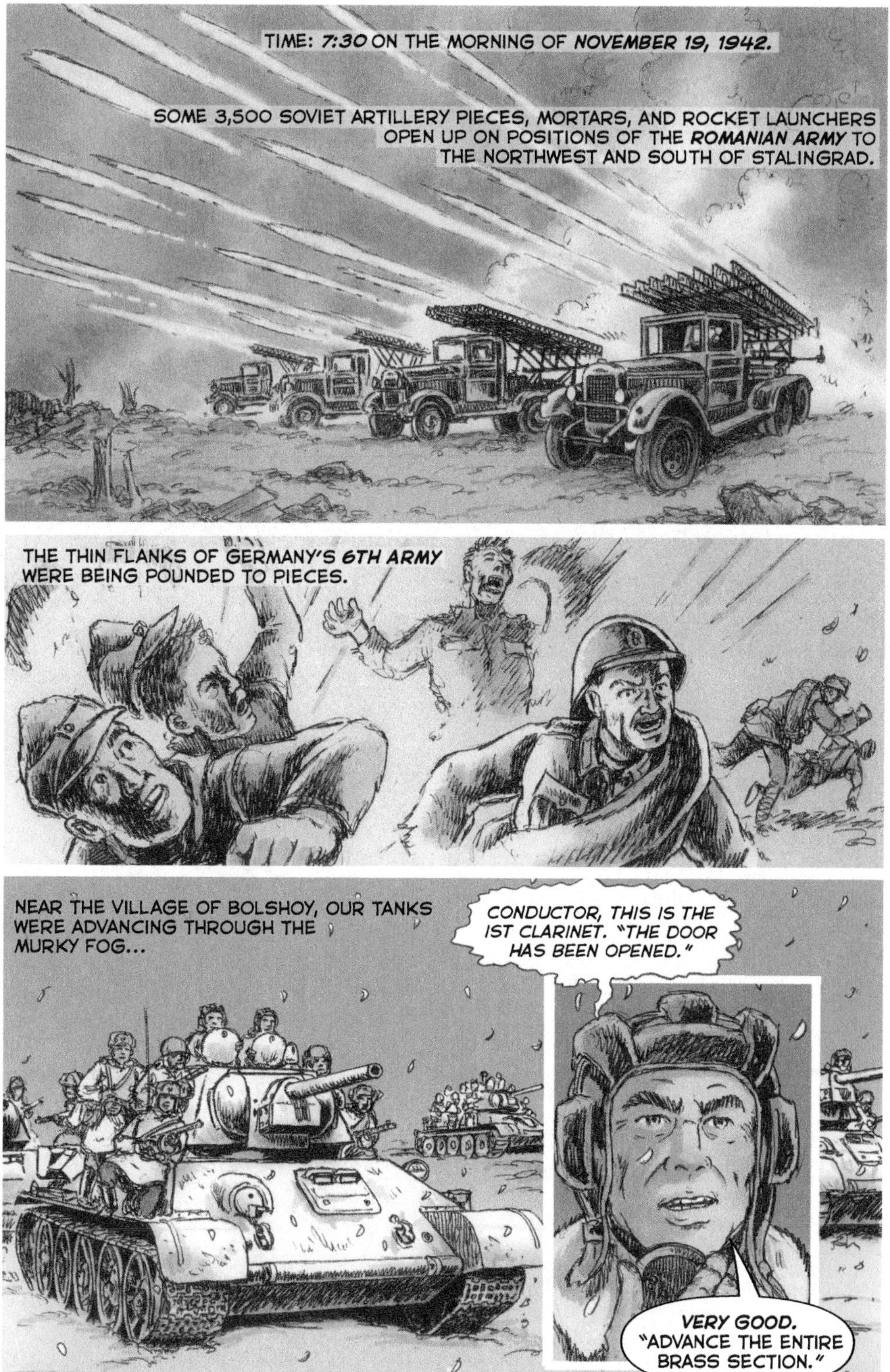
TIME: *7:30* ON THE MORNING OF *NOVEMBER 19, 1942.*
SOME 3,500 SOVIET ARTILLERY PIECES, MORTARS, AND ROCKET LAUNCHERS OPEN UP ON POSITIONS OF THE *ROMANIAN ARMY* TO THE NORTHWEST AND SOUTH OF STALINGRAD.
THE THIN FLANKS OF GERMANY'S *6TH ARMY* WERE BEING POUNDED TO PIECES.
NEAR THE VILLAGE OF BOLSHOY, OUR TANKS WERE ADVANCING THROUGH THE MURKY FOG...
CONDUCTOR, THIS IS THE 1ST CLARINET. "THE DOOR HAS BEEN OPENED."
VERY GOOD. "ADVANCE THE ENTIRE BRASS SECTION."

INFANTRY AND SAPPERS--AS WE CALLED THE ENGINEERS--HAD TAKEN OUT THE FORWARD OUTPOST AND CLEARED OUT THE MINEFIELDS.

THE TANKS ROLLED THROUGH.

CLINGING TO THE BACK OF EACH TANK WERE WHITE-CLAD RUSSIAN SOLDIERS, ALL ARMED WITH *PPSH-41* SUBMACHINE GUNS OR DESTYAREV LIGHT MACHINE GUNS.

ROMANIAN RESISTANCE HAD LITTLE EFFECT ON THE ADVANCE...

MANY RUSSIANS REMEMBER THIS DAY AS THE HAPPIEST DAY OF THE WAR.

THE VIOLATED MOTHERLAND AT LAST WAS AVENGING ITSELF.

THE TOWN OF *OSTROV,* LATE ON THE NIGHT OF *NOVEMBER 21st...*

LOOK, COLONEL! HOW KIND OF THE GERMANS TO LEAVE THESE FOR US--AND IN SUCH GOOD SHAPE!

I BET WE COULD MAKE VERY GOOD USE OF THEM.

BELIEVE ME, WE *WILL.* I HAVE JUST BEEN GIVEN OUR ORDERS--

--THE BRIDGE OVER THE *DON* AT *KALACH!*

KATUSHA, GET ON THE RADIO. I NEED THESE DRIVERS--*ABARCHUK* AND *PERFILEV.*

YES, SIR!

MILLA--CAN YOU DRIVE THAT HALF-TRACK?

SURE!

ALL RIGHT. HERE'S WHAT WE'LL DO...

WE MOVED OUT JUST AFTER MIDNIGHT.

IN THE LEAD WERE THE TWO CAPTURED GERMAN TANKS, THEIR HEADLIGHTS BLAZING...

BEHIND THEM CAME THE HALF-TRACK, WITH MILLA AT THE WHEEL AND KOVCHENKO AND SIX OF HIS MEN ON BOARD.

SIXTEEN *T-34s* FOLLOWED.

I WAS DRIVING OUR TANK, WITH COLONEL NOZDRIN AND MISHA BOVA IN THE TURRET.

THE LIGHT WAS DIM AS WE NEARED THE BRIDGE AT A LITTLE AFTER SIX IN THE MORNING.

THE GERMAN SENTRY, COLD AND TIRED, DIDN'T NOTICE ANYTHING UNUSUAL AS HE WAVED THE TANKS RIGHT ACROSS.

THEN CAPTAIN KOVCHENKO, WEARING A GERMAN HELMET AND SMOKING A GERMAN CIGAR, STUCK HIS HEAD OUT OF THE TOP OF THE HALF-TRACK...

EH--?

...AND CAROMED THE HELMET OFF THE GUARD'S FACE AS WE OPENED FIRE!

⚡UNNGH!⚡

BLANG!

THE UNSUSPECTING *FRITZES* WERE SURPRISED TO BE SHOT BY THEIR OWN *PANZERS!*

OUR SIXTEEN *T-34*s WERE LINED UP ON THE WEST BANK, FIRING ON ANYTHING THAT TRIED TO SUPPORT THE DEFENSE OF THE BRIDGE.

IT WAS SOON OVER. I LEAPT FROM OUR TANK, ELATED.

REMEMBER, KATUSHA? THIS IS THAT SAME BRIDGE WE CROSSED WITH TARAS LAST YEAR--!

AND WE'VE MANAGED TO TAKE IT WITHOUT LOSING A SINGLE MAN!

AH--IT *DID* SEEM FAMILIAR!

WHAT A DAY! WHAT A DAY!

AND WHAT DO *YOU* THINK ABOUT IT, LITTLE TYMOSHENKO?

WELL...THIS IS SURELY SOMETHING TO WRITE HOME ABOUT TO YOUR WIFE, CAPTAIN!

BUT THEN HIS FACE FELL, AS IF ALL THE LIFE HAD SUDDENLY WASHED OUT OF IT...

NO. YOU SEE... LAST WINTER, MY WIFE *DIED*--IN LENINGRAD...

SHE--AND OUR THREE DAUGHTERS-- STARVED TO DEATH.

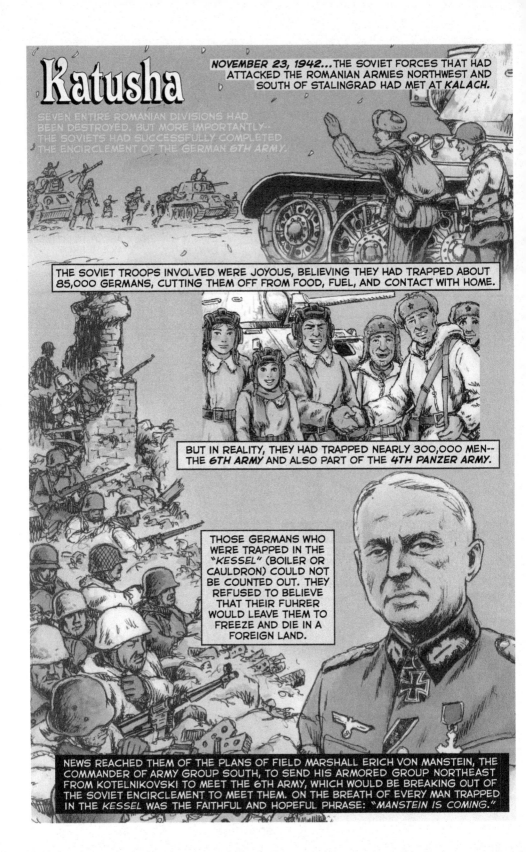

Katusha

NOVEMBER 23, 1942... THE SOVIET FORCES THAT HAD ATTACKED THE ROMANIAN ARMIES NORTHWEST AND SOUTH OF STALINGRAD HAD MET AT *KALACH.*

SEVEN ENTIRE ROMANIAN DIVISIONS HAD BEEN DESTROYED. BUT MORE IMPORTANTLY-- THE SOVIETS HAD SUCCESSFULLY COMPLETED THE ENCIRCLEMENT OF THE GERMAN *6TH ARMY.*

THE SOVIET TROOPS INVOLVED WERE JOYOUS, BELIEVING THEY HAD TRAPPED ABOUT 85,000 GERMANS, CUTTING THEM OFF FROM FOOD, FUEL, AND CONTACT WITH HOME.

BUT IN REALITY, THEY HAD TRAPPED NEARLY 300,000 MEN-- THE *6TH ARMY* AND ALSO PART OF THE *4TH PANZER ARMY.*

THOSE GERMANS WHO WERE TRAPPED IN THE *"KESSEL"* (BOILER OR CAULDRON) COULD NOT BE COUNTED OUT. THEY REFUSED TO BELIEVE THAT THEIR FUHRER WOULD LEAVE THEM TO FREEZE AND DIE IN A FOREIGN LAND.

NEWS REACHED THEM OF THE PLANS OF FIELD MARSHALL ERICH VON MANSTEIN, THE COMMANDER OF ARMY GROUP SOUTH, TO SEND HIS ARMORED GROUP NORTHEAST FROM KOTELNIKOVSKI TO MEET THE 6TH ARMY, WHICH WOULD BE BREAKING OUT OF THE SOVIET ENCIRCLEMENT TO MEET THEM. ON THE BREATH OF EVERY MAN TRAPPED IN THE *KESSEL* WAS THE FAITHFUL AND HOPEFUL PHRASE: *"MANSTEIN IS COMING."*

ARENA

I CAN'T REMEMBER THE NAME OF THE TOWN--I DOUBT THAT ANY OF US COULD. I JUST REMEMBER IT AS "TWO CHURCHES" BECAUSE--WELL, THERE WERE TWO VERY PRETTY CHURCHES THERE...

AS SOON AS WE REALIZED *MANSTEIN* HAD LAUNCHED AN OFFENSIVE TO RELIEVE STALINGRAD, WE LAUNCHED OUR OWN OFFENSIVE TO STOP HIM (WHEN I SAY "WE," I MEAN ME AND THE GENERALS, *HA!*).

IT WAS CALLED *OPERATION LITTLE SATURN.* THEY CALLED IT THAT BECAUSE OUR OFFENSIVE TO SURROUND STALINGRAD HAD BEEN CODE-NAMED *OPERATION URANUS.* BACK THEN IN THOSE DAYS, THE SOVIETS SEEMED TO HAVE A FIXATION ON PLANETS--AS IF IT COULD MAKE US SOUND MORE EDUCATED THAN WE REALLY WERE.

AHA...! SUKHANOV IS SIGNALLING.

HE SAYS CAPTAIN KOVCHENKO JUST CALLED DOWN FROM THE TOWER TO REPORT THERE ARE NO GERMANS--ONLY FIELDS AND BIRCH WOODS.

HA! I CAN SEE HIM!

WHAT'S HE DOING?

HERE-- LOOK FOR YOURSELF!

OH, MY HERO!

IF ONLY HE WERE WAVING AT *ME...!*

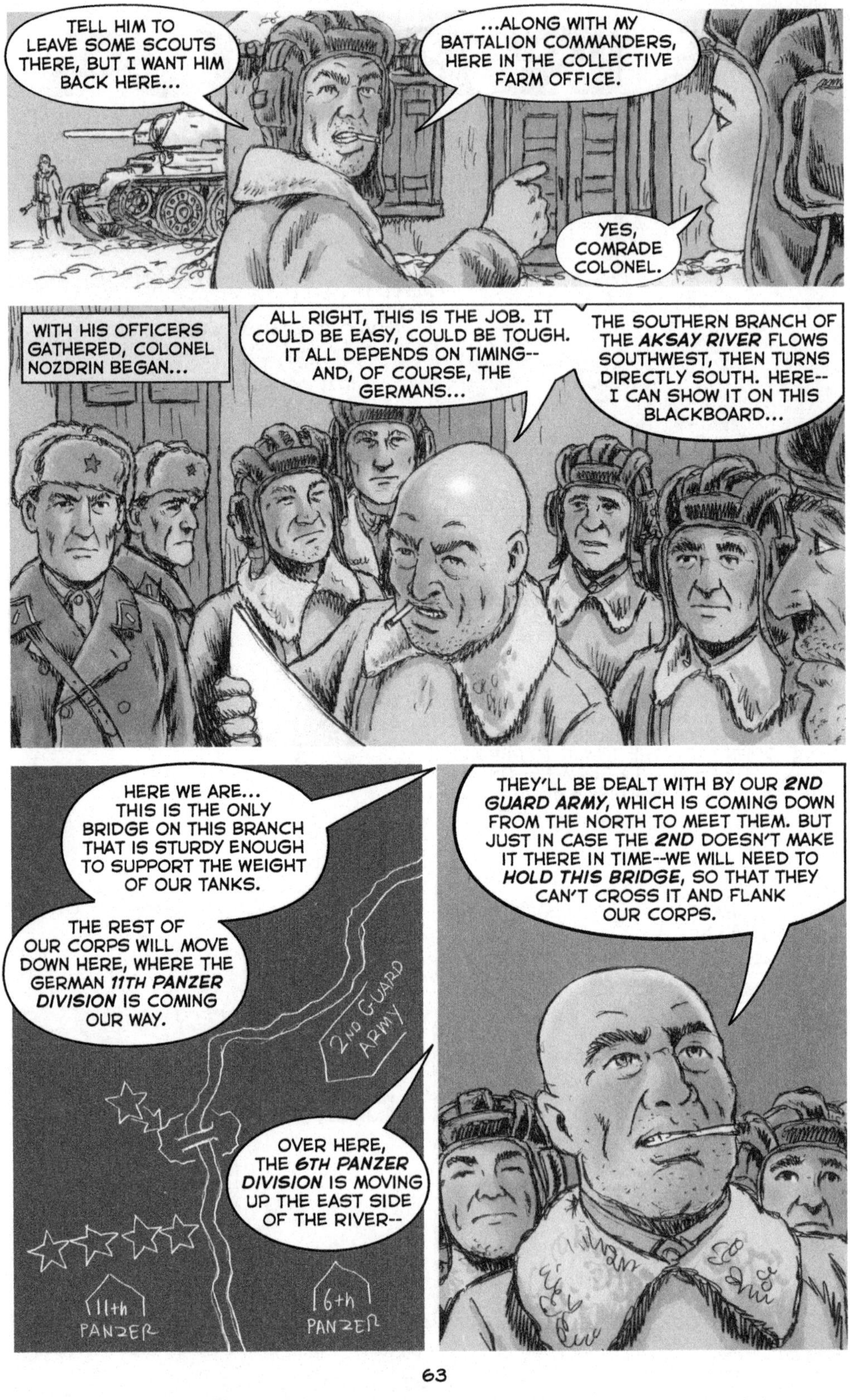
TELL HIM TO LEAVE SOME SCOUTS THERE, BUT I WANT HIM BACK HERE...
...ALONG WITH MY BATTALION COMMANDERS, HERE IN THE COLLECTIVE FARM OFFICE.
YES, COMRADE COLONEL.
WITH HIS OFFICERS GATHERED, COLONEL NOZDRIN BEGAN...
ALL RIGHT, THIS IS THE JOB. IT COULD BE EASY, COULD BE TOUGH. IT ALL DEPENDS ON TIMING--AND, OF COURSE, THE GERMANS...
THE SOUTHERN BRANCH OF THE *AKSAY RIVER* FLOWS SOUTHWEST, THEN TURNS DIRECTLY SOUTH. HERE--I CAN SHOW IT ON THIS BLACKBOARD...
HERE WE ARE... THIS IS THE ONLY BRIDGE ON THIS BRANCH THAT IS STURDY ENOUGH TO SUPPORT THE WEIGHT OF OUR TANKS.
THE REST OF OUR CORPS WILL MOVE DOWN HERE, WHERE THE GERMAN *11TH PANZER DIVISION* IS COMING OUR WAY.
2ND GUARD ARMY
OVER HERE, THE *6TH PANZER DIVISION* IS MOVING UP THE EAST SIDE OF THE RIVER--
11th PANZER
6th PANZER
THEY'LL BE DEALT WITH BY OUR *2ND GUARD ARMY*, WHICH IS COMING DOWN FROM THE NORTH TO MEET THEM. BUT JUST IN CASE THE *2ND* DOESN'T MAKE IT THERE IN TIME--WE WILL NEED TO *HOLD THIS BRIDGE*, SO THAT THEY CAN'T CROSS IT AND FLANK OUR CORPS.

NOGIN AND GUCHKOV--I WANT YOUR TANK BATTALIONS ACROSS THE RIVER AND INTO THE TOWN. DON'T DIG THEM IN--HIDE THEM INSIDE THE BARNS, HAYSTACKS--OR EVEN IN HOUSES. I'LL BE CHECKING ON THEM LATER.

MIRONOV, KEEP YOUR BATTALION UP HERE OVERLOOKING THE RIVER, BUT I WANT YOUR TANKS DUG IN.

KOLYA--ANY CIVILIANS LEFT IN TOWN?

I DIDN'T SEE ANY--BUT THERE ARE ALWAYS A FEW WHO STAY BEHIND.

I WANT TWO OF YOUR INFANTRY COMPANIES IN TOWN. DIG THEM INTO THE CELLARS. YOU KNOW WHAT I WANT.

RIGHT. IT MIGHT BE A GOOD IDEA TO PUT A FEW SCOUTS BACK IN THOSE BIRCHES OVER ON THE OTHER SIDE OF THE FIELD.

GOOD IDEA.

WHAT ABOUT US, COLONEL?

DIG THE TANK IN, BUT DON'T BOTHER MAKING ROOM UNDERNEATH IT. ONE MAN CAN STAY WITH WITH THE TANK, AND ROTATE THE OTHERS INSIDE.

YES, SIR!

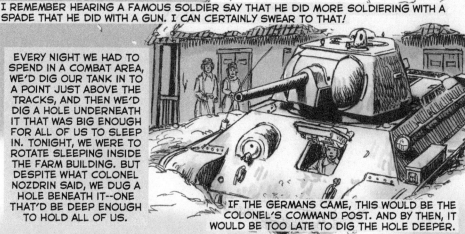

I REMEMBER HEARING A FAMOUS SOLDIER SAY THAT HE DID MORE SOLDIERING WITH A SPADE THAT HE DID WITH A GUN. I CAN CERTAINLY SWEAR TO THAT!

EVERY NIGHT WE HAD TO SPEND IN A COMBAT AREA, WE'D DIG OUR TANK IN TO A POINT JUST ABOVE THE TRACKS, AND THEN WE'D DIG A HOLE UNDERNEATH IT THAT WAS BIG ENOUGH FOR ALL OF US TO SLEEP IN. TONIGHT, WE WERE TO ROTATE SLEEPING INSIDE THE FARM BUILDING. BUT DESPITE WHAT COLONEL NOZDRIN SAID, WE DUG A HOLE BENEATH IT--ONE THAT'D BE DEEP ENOUGH TO HOLD ALL OF US.

IF THE GERMANS CAME, THIS WOULD BE THE COLONEL'S COMMAND POST. AND BY THEN, IT WOULD BE TOO LATE TO DIG THE HOLE DEEPER.

A FEW MILES TO THE SOUTH, GERMAN MECHANIZED INFANTRY WERE STEADILY MOVING THROUGH THE SLUSHY SNOW...

THESE MODERN CAVALRYMEN LONG AGO HAD LEARNED TO SLEEP ON THE MOVE, DESPITE BEING KNOCKED AGAINST THE STEEL HULL OR THEIR ALSO-SLEEPING FRIENDS...

THEY'D ALSO LEARNED TO IMMEDIATELY AWAKEN TO THE SOUND OF APPROACHING DANGER.

WAS IST--?

EH--?

FROM OVER A NEARBY HILL ROARED A TERRIFYING SCENE WHICH COULD HAVE COME FROM CENTURIES PAST--MEN AND HORSES OF A *COSSACK CAVALRY UNIT* SURGED DOWN UPON THE GERMAN FORCES.

THE COSSACKS HAD PROVED TO BE EFFECTIVE IN RECONNAISSANCE AND PARTISAN ROLES...

...BUT *LESS SO* AGAINST ARMORED FORCES.

THE *PANZERGRENADIERS* IMMEDIATELY DISMOUNTED AND FORMED A LINE WITH THEIR VEHICLES, WHICH THEY TURNED TO FACE THE ONSLAUGHT.

THE GERMANS PREPARED THEIR WEAPONS...

...AND CALMLY WAITED FOR THE ENEMY TO COME INTO RANGE...

THEN--

--THEY UNLEASHED A RAIN OF *LEADEN HELLFIRE!!*

SUDDENLY... ...ANOTHER ELEMENT CAME INTO PLAY!

THE GERMANS WERE JUBILANT TO SEE THEIR *PANZERS* ARRIVE!

WITH THEIR SUPERIOR FIREPOWER... ...THE TANKS MADE SHORT WORK OF IT.

ACH...!

I HATE TO SEE THESE FINE, NOBLE ANIMALS SUFFER IN THIS WAY...

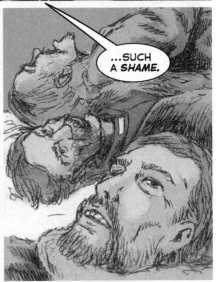

...SUCH A *SHAME*.

67

KATUSHA! WAKE UP!

¿MMRF...?¿

...YOU'RE EARLY--HOW COME?

WHY QUESTION GOOD FORTUNE? YOU CAN GO INSIDE NOW, WHERE IT'S NICE AND WARM.

MMMOKAY...

AH! COME ON IN, LITTLE TYMOSHENKO!

WHY... THANK YOU, COMRADE.

I MUST SAY, IT SEEMS YOU AND YOUR SISTER HAVE ADAPTED TO OUTDOOR LIFE BETTER THAN MOST OF MY INFANTRYMEN!

WELL, OUR UNCLE TARAS TAUGHT US HOW TO LIVE UNDER DIFFICULT SITUATIONS...

...BUT MORE IMPORTANTLY, HE TAUGHT US HOW IT JUST MAKES THINGS WORSE TO COMPLAIN.

HA! NOW THAT IS A LESSON FOR THE ARMY!

THE BRIGADE POLITICAL OFFICER SAT OFF IN THE CORNER. I WHISPERED TO KOVCHENKO...

AH, IT'S COMRADE CHEKOV...

HE'S ALWAYS SEEMED ODD TO ME--A BIT SCARY.

STEPHAN? OH, HE'S ALL RIGHT--A PRODUCT OF HIS ENVIRONMENT. THE POOR MAN IS AN ORPHAN OF THE REVOLUTION.

WHAT?

"HIS FIRST MEMORIES ARE OF BEING ALONE ON THE STREETS. HE KNOWS NOTHING OF HIS PARENTS--ALL HE EVER HAD OF HIS OWN WAS THE *REVOLUTION*...

Тульская Комсомольской

"HIS ONLY MOTHER IS *RUSSIA*... AND HIS FATHER IS THE *PARTY*."

OH. HOW *SAD* FOR HIM...

I...I WANT TO APOLOGIZE TO *YOU*, FOR WHAT I SAID ABOUT WRITING TO YOUR WIFE... YOU SEE...I--

--I HAD NO IDEA.

CAPTAIN KOVCHENKO DIDN'T SAY ANYTHING FOR A MOMENT.

WHEN HE SPOKE, HIS VOICE WAS *HUSHED*...

LARYISSA... WAS A RATHER FRAGILE GIRL... THE BIRTH OF OUR THIRD DAUGHTER TOOK A LOT OUT OF HER. SHE--SHE WAS MUCH TOO WEAK TO GO THROUGH THAT *WINTER*... AND-- AND OUR *LITTLE GIRLS*--!

THE WORDS CAUGHT IN HIS THROAT. HE SWALLOWED HARD--AND WENT ON...

YOU KNOW... I KNOW THEY ARE *GONE*. THOSE WHO TOLD ME WOULD NOT HAVE LIED TO ME. BUT DEEP DOWN--I JUST *CANNOT BELIEVE* IT!

HERE, WITHIN MY BRAIN--I *KNOW* THEY'RE GONE...BUT--!

BUT--YOU CANNOT BELIEVE IT IN *HERE*...

KOVCHENKO SIGHED SOFTLY AND NODDED.

69

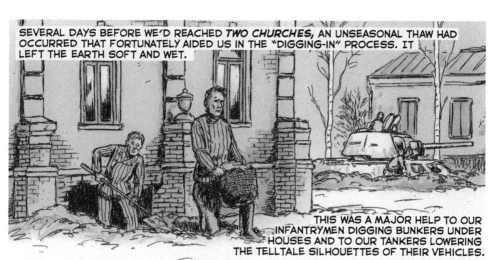

SEVERAL DAYS BEFORE WE'D REACHED *TWO CHURCHES*, AN UNSEASONAL THAW HAD OCCURRED THAT FORTUNATELY AIDED US IN THE "DIGGING-IN" PROCESS. IT LEFT THE EARTH SOFT AND WET.

THIS WAS A MAJOR HELP TO OUR INFANTRYMEN DIGGING BUNKERS UNDER HOUSES AND TO OUR TANKERS LOWERING THE TELLTALE SILHOUETTES OF THEIR VEHICLES.

THEN, AS IF BY MAGIC--THE FRIGID NORTH WIND RETURNED, FREEZING THE GROUND AND HARDENING OUR ARTIFICIAL BARRIERS.

AH, HAHAHA! YES!

THIS IS WHAT MAKES IGLOOS SO STRONG!

COLONEL NOZDRIN TRULY HAD AN EYE FOR THE LAND. HE PREPARED OUR POSITION SO WE'D BE READY FOR A LONG, DIFFICULT DEFENSE-- OR A QUICK PULLOUT.

HE WOULD STAND AROUND HOLDING A LONG STICK AS HE TALKED WITH SOLDIERS ABOUT ANYTHING AND EVERYTHING.

BUT WHILE HE TALKED, HIS MIND WAS WORKING...

...ROLLING THINGS OVER...

...ASKING HIMSELF QUESTIONS...

...AND SOLVING PROBLEMS.

TWO DAYS LATER, A SMALL VEHICLE APPROACHED OUR CAMP FROM THE EAST.

WE ALREADY KNEW OF ITS COMING BEFORE IT WAS IN SIGHT--ONE OF OUR SCOUTS UP IN THE BIRCH WOODS SAW THEM AND SIGNALLED THE NEWS TO US WITH A FLASHLIGHT.

IT WAS A SMALL GERMAN HALF-TRACK, A *SDKFZ 250.*

THERE WERE FIVE MEN IN IT. THEY DROVE INTO THE VILLAGE AS IF THEY WERE TOURISTS LOOKING FOR A SUITABLE HOTEL ON THE PRYMORSKY BOULEVARD IN ODESSA.

THEY HAD NO IDEA HOW MANY *GUNS* WERE TRAINED ON THEM.

HMM... I DON'T SEE ANYBODY.

WELL, I SEE SMOKE FROM A FEW CHIMNEYS. *HA,* WE'RE JUST IN TIME FOR *BREAKFAST!*

LOOK! HERE COMES AN OLD MAN WITH A BASKET OF TREATS FOR US!

KIRK, CAN'T YOU THINK OF ANYTHING BUT *FOOD?*

HOLD UP, OLD MAN! WHAT DO YOU HAVE THERE IN YOUR BASKET?

THE OLD MAN STOPPED AND TURNED, APPARENTLY FRIGHTENED...

THE GERMAN CALLED *KIRK* WRESTED THE BASKET FROM THE OLD MAN'S HAND...

NO! THERE'S NOT ENOUGH FOR *ALL* OF YOU!

BUT THERE'S JUST THE *FIVE* OF US, OLD MAN!

JUST *FIVE* OF YOU!

THE OLD MAN'S LOUD STATEMENT WAS A FACT--NOT A QUESTION.

THEN, FROM OUT OF NOWHERE...

FOUR SHOTS RANG OUT SO FAST THEY SOUNDED AS *ONE.*

KIRK TURNED...

...AND SAW HIS FOUR COMPANIONS LYING IN THE SNOW--ALL *DEAD* WITHIN AN INSTANT.

HE LOOKED BACK AT THE OLD MAN--AND SAW HIM SUDDENLY STANDING SEVERAL METERS AWAY FROM WHERE HE HAD BEEN.

HUH...?

THE OLD MAN WAS *SMILING.*

KIRK HAD NO INKLING THIS "OLD MAN" WAS REALLY OUR *SENIOR SERGEANT GENRIKH DYATLONKO,* RECIPIENT OF THE ST. GEORGE'S CROSS DURING THE GREAT WAR.

KIRK LOOKED DOWN AT THE BASKET IN HIS HAND IN DAWNING *HORROR...*

THE LAST THOUGHT THAT KIRK EVER HAD--

?

--WAS THAT SOMEONE HAD TAKEN HIS BASKET.

EXCELLENT WORK, GENRIKH!

HEH!

NOW--GET THOSE BODIES OUT OF HERE.

PETROV, DRIVE THEIR HALF-TRACK UP THE HILL, AND PARK IT BEHIND THE FARM OFFICE.

IN JUST A FEW MINUTES...

...NOT A TRACE REMAINED TO SHOW THAT ANYTHING UNUSUAL HAD HAPPENED IN THE VILLAGE SQUARE.

NOW IT WAS TIME TO *WAIT*...

COLONEL NOZDRIN POSITIONED HIMSELF OUTSIDE, WHERE HE COULD DIRECT THE ACTION. HE KEPT ME BY THE RADIO, JUST IN CASE. I SAT IN THE DRIVER'S SEAT SO I COULD SEE OUT THE FORWARD HATCH.

MILLA STOOD UP IN THE TURRET WITH MISHA BOVA, PREPARED TO ACT AS HIS LOADER, IF NECESSARY.

73

WITH THE FEW WOMEN IN OUR UNIT ALONGSIDE ALL THESE MEN, YOU MIGHT WONDER WHY THERE WASN'T MORE--WELL... SEXUAL ACTIVITY GOING ON.

AT THE FRONT, COMBAT UNITS WERE KEPT EXTREMELY BUSY. SLEEP--TRULY *DEEP* SLEEP-- WAS A VERY ELUSIVE LUXURY.

SO IN REALITY, THERE JUST WASN'T ENOUGH *TIME.* BESIDES, PEOPLE OFTEN WERE JUST TOO DOG-TIRED TO EVEN *THINK* ABOUT IT.

BUT... IT *DID* HAPPEN.

MANY HIGH-LEVEL OFFICERS KEPT WHAT WERE CALLED "CAMP WIVES." TAKE, FOR INSTANCE, THE COLONEL'S DRIVER, *VERA FYODOROVICH...*

COLONEL NOZDRIN WAS MARRIED, IN FACT-- AND HAD A SON WHO WAS A PILOT. BUT IT WAS QUITE OBVIOUS TO ALL OF US THAT VERA SERVED AS HIS "CAMP WIFE." OF COURSE, NOBODY EVER SPOKE OF IT ABOVE A WHISPER--STILL, WE ALL ACCEPTED IT.

EVERYONE LOVED THE GIRL MEDICS. WHEN OUR GALINA MIKHAYLOVA PULLED ALEX FOMICHEVA FROM HIS BURNING TANK, HE SWORE TO HER HIS LOVE FOREVER...

...AND HE KEPT THAT VOW, TOO--ALEX FOMICHEVA WAS KILLED AT PROKHOROVKA.

I FELT A LITTLE SORRY FOR MISHA--HE CLEARLY LIKED MILLA. BUT MILLA ONLY HAD FEELINGS FOR UNCLE TARAS.

I GUESS THAT'S JUST THE WAY THINGS ARE.

BUT NOBODY AS YET HAD BOTHERED *ME.*

I WAS ONLY BOTHERED BY MY *OWN FEELINGS.*

NEAR NOON, SCOUTS IN THE BIRCH WOOD HEARD ROARING MOTORS AND CLANKING TRACKS.

SOON WE SAW ABOUT A DOZEN GERMAN HALF-TRACKS WHEELING INTO OUR VIEW. THEY TRUNDLED ACROSS THE SNOWY FIELDS... AND THEN--

--HEADED STRAIGHT FOR *TWO CHURCHES.*

WELL, HERE THEY COME--I HOPE EVERYONE IS *READY...!*

I KNEW CAPTAIN KOVCHENKO WAS READY... HE WAS *ALWAYS* READY FOR COMBAT.

THIS GROUP DID NOT ROLL IN FULL OF BRASH OVERCONFIDENCE LIKE OUR PREVIOUS VISITORS HAD. THESE HALF-TRACKS MOVED INTO A STAGGERED-LINE FORMATION--

--AND THEN THEY *STOPPED.*

THE *PANZERGRENADIERS* WERE DISGORGED FROM THE VEHICLES TO FORM A BATTLE LINE ACROSS THE WIDTH OF THE VILLAGE.

...THEN, PROMPTED BY A SIGNAL BLOWN ON A WHISTLE, THEY BEGAN THEIR *ADVANCE.*

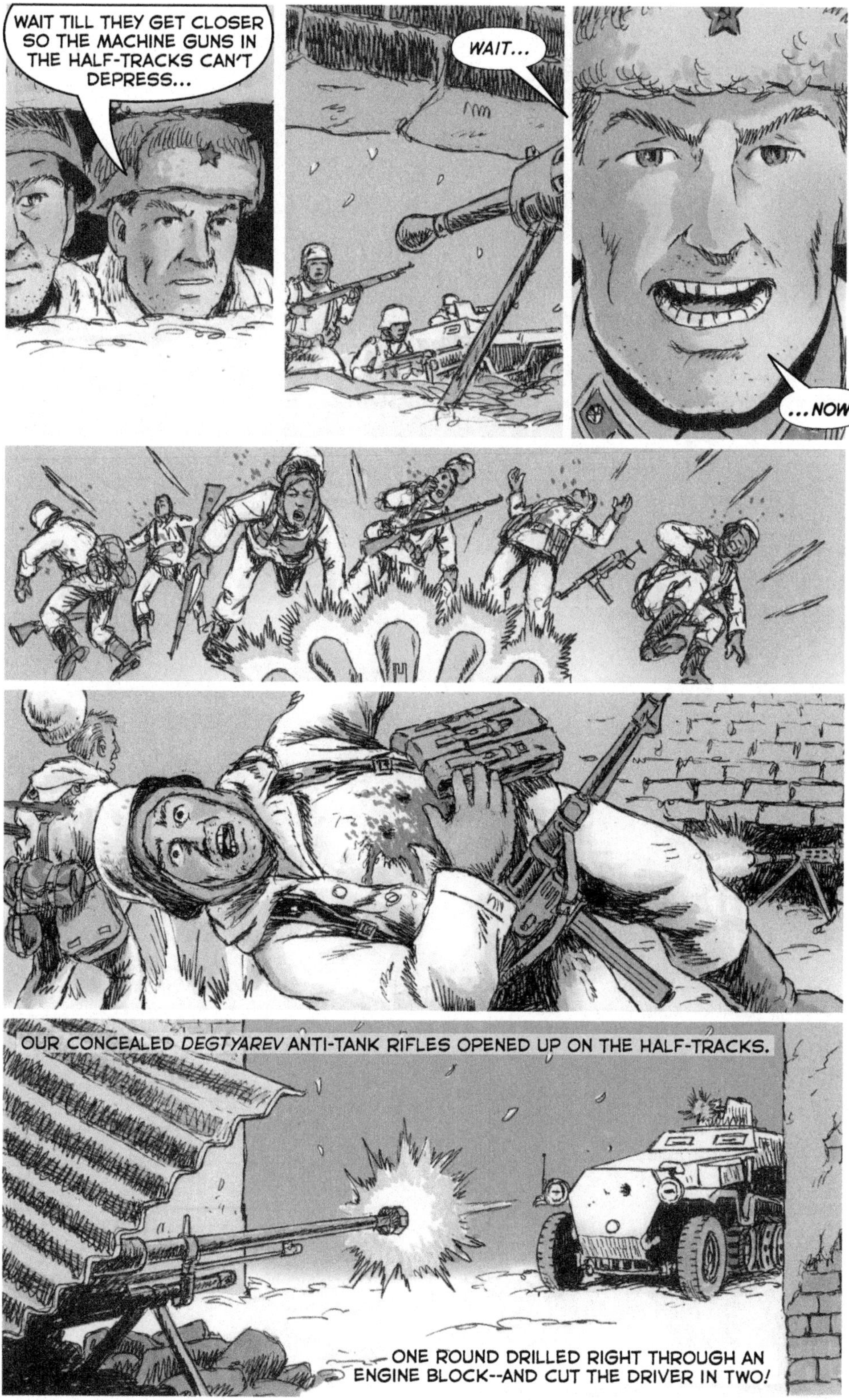
WAIT TILL THEY GET CLOSER SO THE MACHINE GUNS IN THE HALF-TRACKS CAN'T DEPRESS...
WAIT...
...NOW.
OUR CONCEALED *DEGTYAREV* ANTI-TANK RIFLES OPENED UP ON THE HALF-TRACKS.
ONE ROUND DRILLED RIGHT THROUGH AN ENGINE BLOCK--AND CUT THE DRIVER IN TWO!

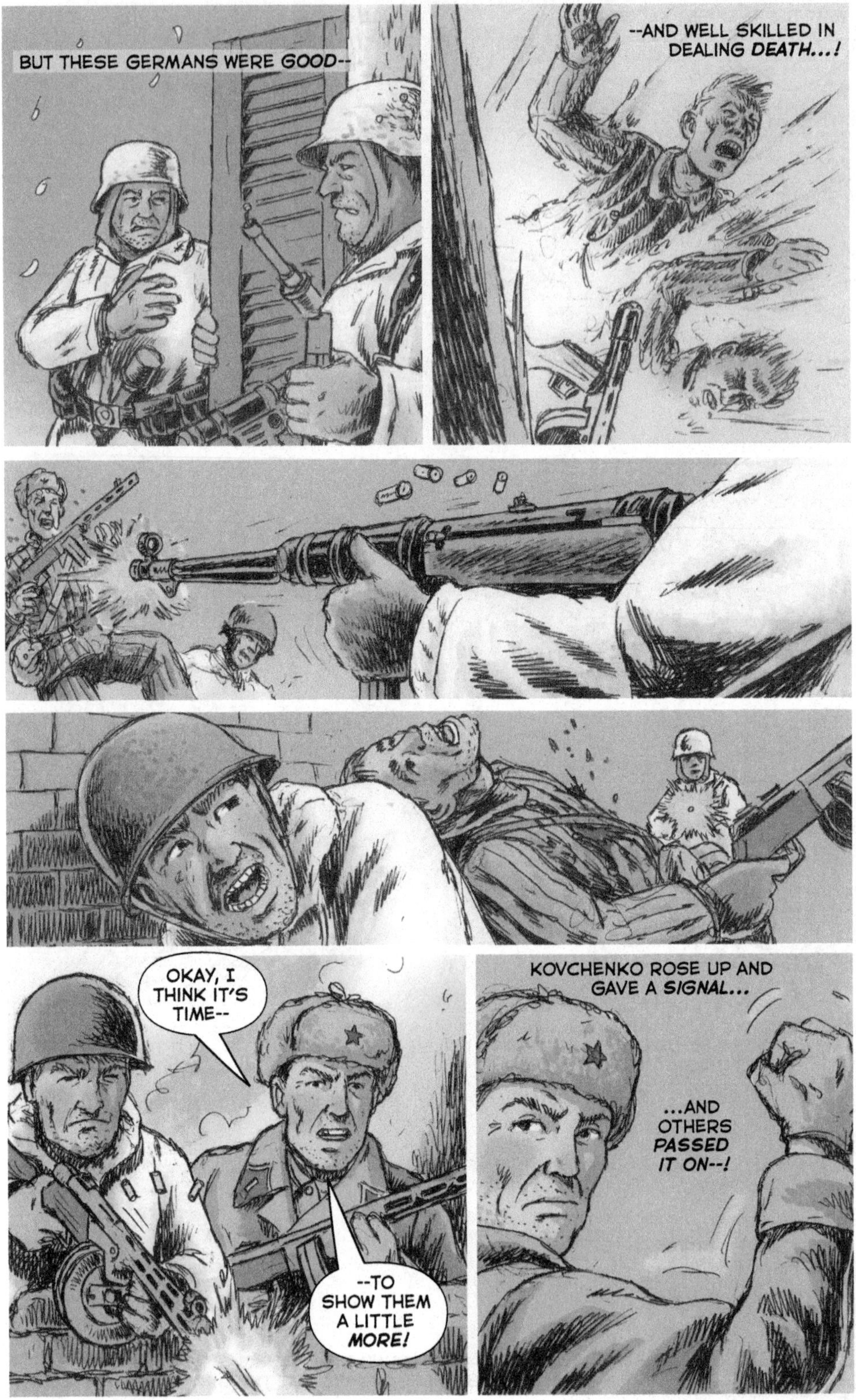
BUT THESE GERMANS WERE GOOD--
--AND WELL SKILLED IN DEALING DEATH...!
OKAY, I THINK IT'S TIME--
--TO SHOW THEM A LITTLE MORE!
KOVCHENKO ROSE UP AND GAVE A SIGNAL...
...AND OTHERS PASSED IT ON--!

A SINGLE *T-34* TANK ROLLED OUT FROM BEHIND A BUILDING...

...TWO MORE EXPOSED THEMSELVES FROM BENEATH THE HAYSTACKS...

THEY DROVE INTO THE FIELD AND FORMED ALONG THE GERMANS' FLANK...

...AS *THREE MORE* PULLED OUT ONTO THE FAR SIDE...!

UH--?!

ACH, SCHEISS!!

...AND THEN THEY ENGAGED THEIR *STUNNED ENEMIES!*

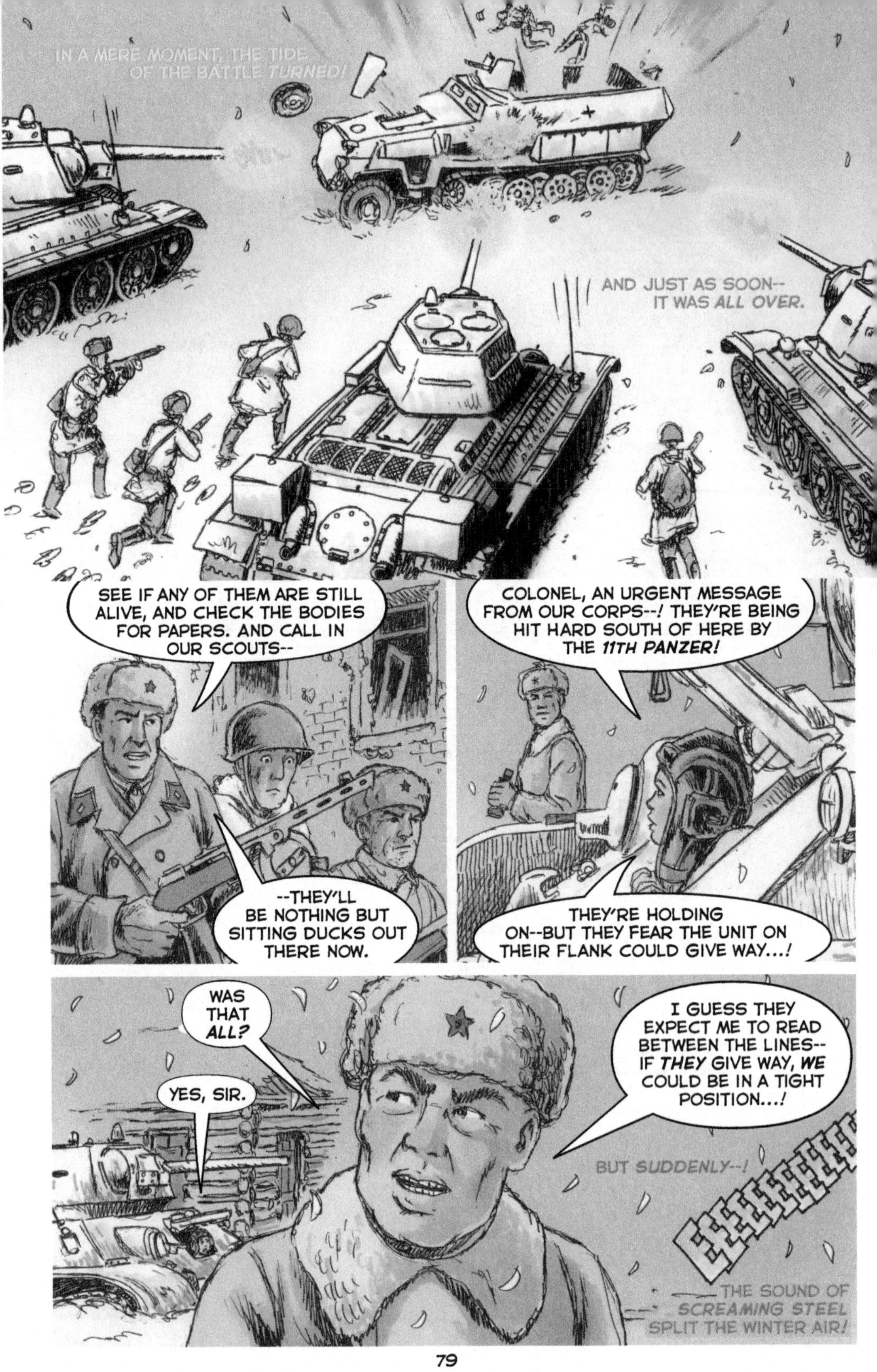
IN A MERE MOMENT, THE TIDE OF THE BATTLE TURNED!
AND JUST AS SOON-- IT WAS ALL OVER.
SEE IF ANY OF THEM ARE STILL ALIVE, AND CHECK THE BODIES FOR PAPERS. AND CALL IN OUR SCOUTS--
--THEY'LL BE NOTHING BUT SITTING DUCKS OUT THERE NOW.
COLONEL, AN URGENT MESSAGE FROM OUR CORPS--! THEY'RE BEING HIT HARD SOUTH OF HERE BY THE 11TH PANZER!
THEY'RE HOLDING ON--BUT THEY FEAR THE UNIT ON THEIR FLANK COULD GIVE WAY...!
WAS THAT ALL?
YES, SIR.
I GUESS THEY EXPECT ME TO READ BETWEEN THE LINES-- IF THEY GIVE WAY, WE COULD BE IN A TIGHT POSITION...!
BUT SUDDENLY--!
EEEEEEEEEE
--THE SOUND OF SCREAMING STEEL SPLIT THE WINTER AIR!

I'LL GET UNDER THE TANK! YOU CLOSE UP THAT HATCH!

AS I SHUT THE HATCH, I THANKED MY LUCKY STARS I'D DUG OUT THAT BUNKER BENEATH OUR TANK!

MOVE IT! QUICK!!

-I'M TRYIN', I'M TRYIN'--!!

THE BUNKERS UNDER THE HOUSES AFFORDED GOOD PROTECTION...

...BUT UNFORTUNATELY--*NOT* IN THE EVENT OF A *DIRECT HIT!*

THE BOMBARDMENT ENDED JUST AS QUICKLY AS IT HAD BEGUN.

EVERYBODY UP! CLEAR YOUR FIELDS OF FIRE--THEY'LL BE RIGHT *ON US!*

GET THE *WOUNDED* BACK UP THE HILL!

QUICKLY! BEFORE ANOTHER *BARRAGE BEGINS!*

WHERE'S *SHIRAKOV?*

HE'S *DEAD!* SHELLS CAUGHT US OUT IN THE OPEN--!!

CAPTAIN, I SAW MORE *TANKS!* THEY'RE BEHIND THOSE TREES, HEADING THIS WAY!

THEY'RE RIGHT ON *MY HEELS*--!!

SERGEYEV! GET THIS MAN UP THE HILL, WITH THE REST OF THE WOUNDED!

HEAR THAT *SOUND,* CAPTAIN--?! SHOULD WE GET OUR TANKS BACK UNDER COVER?

DON'T BOTHER, GENRIKH--IT'S FAR *TOO LATE* TO TRY TO FOOL THEM *NOW.*

81

OUT OF THE SMOKE AND BLOWING SNOW EMERGED GERMAN TANKS CAMOUFLAGED WITH JAGGED, ANGULAR LINES. AS WE HAD DONE WITH OUR TANKS, THESE WERE RANDOMLY SPLATTERED WITH WHITE PAINT TO PROVIDE CONCEALMENT IN THE WINTER LANDSCAPE-- BUT ALL IT ACCOMPLISHED WAS TO MAKE THEM LOOK LIKE EVEN MORE FEARSOME AND PROFICIENT INSTRUMENTS OF MURDER.

EH? THOSE PANZER IVs SEEM TO HAVE LONGER CANNONS...?!

OUR INFANTRYMEN INSTINCTIVELY BACKED OFF INTO THE VILLAGE, WHILE OUR TANKS ROLLED OUT TO MEET THE ENEMY.

ANY DISCUSSION OF CANNON-MUZZLE VELOCITY OR ARMOR STRENGTH WAS BESIDE THE POINT HERE...

...AT A RANGE THIS CLOSE, ALL ORDNANCE WAS *DEADLY*--

--AND *ALL* ARMOR *FAILED.*

BOTH SIDES WERE EXPLOITING THE LAYOUT OF THE BUILDINGS, AS IF THE WHOLE TOWN WERE SOME GIANT MAZE...

THE COLONEL SEEMED TENSE AND RIGID, BUT ABSOLUTELY FOCUSED ON THE JOB AT HAND.

THEY REALLY WANT TO TAKE THAT BRIDGE...

WELL, THEN, WHY DON'T WE JUST *BLOW* IT *UP*?

MUCH TOO LATE, I BIT MY TONGUE. IMAGINE LOWLY ME, ADVISING THE BRIGADE COMMANDER--! I FULLY EXPECTED COLONEL NOZDRIN'S RIGHTEOUS WRATH TO POUR DOWN UPON ME. INSTEAD, HE REPLIED IN A CALM, SOOTHING VOICE...

NO, KATUSHA. WE HAVE GOT TO *DEFEND* THE BRIDGE, NOT BLOW IT UP.

BUT I COULD SEE TENSION PULL THE MUSCLES OF HIS NECK AS HE WATCHED THE CAULDRON BELOW...

...THEN HE'D LOOK TO THE SOUTH, AS HE WONDERED WHETHER HIS CORPS WERE HOLDING OUT AGAINST THE *11TH PANZER*...

...THEN HE WOULD LOOK TO THE NORTHEAST, CURSING UNDER HIS BREATH--

--WHERE IS THE *2ND GUARD ARMY*...?!!

I LOOKED DOWN AT THE BOILING KETTLE BELOW...AND REFLECTED THAT IF IT COULD BE FROZEN IN TIME, AND IF THE UNIFORMS AND MOUNTS AND WEAPONS EXCHANGED, THIS AWFUL TABLEAU COULD BE REPRESENTATIONAL OF *POLTAVA* OR *BORODINO*--OR, EVEN FARTHER FLUNG, OF *WATERLOO* OR *GETTYSBURG...*

...OR EVEN *HELL!*

IT WAS UNBEARABLY *NOISY*, TOO. AUTOMATIC WEAPONSFIRE COMPETED WITH HIGH-VELOCITY CANNON BLASTS, AND WHATEVER SHORT PAUSE IN BETWEEN THAT COULD BE CALLED A LULL WAS FILLED WITH SCREAMS AND CURSES.

TANKS FOUGHT SO CLOSE TOGETHER THAT THE BLAST OF ONE GUN WAS UNDISTINGUISHABLE FROM THE IMPACT ON ITS TARGET.

FROM THE TOP OF THE HILL, I COULD SEE MEN GETTING BLOWN APART--

--ONLY TO HEAR THE SOUND OF THE KILLING WEAPON AS IT REACHED MY EARS A SPLIT SECOND LATER.

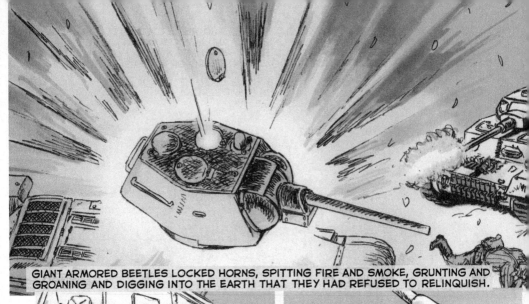

GIANT ARMORED BEETLES LOCKED HORNS, SPITTING FIRE AND SMOKE, GRUNTING AND GROANING AND DIGGING INTO THE EARTH THAT THEY HAD REFUSED TO RELINQUISH.

AROUND THEIR CLAWING, DEADLY FEET, THE WARRIOR ANTS STRUGGLED--

--THEIR ENDEAVORS NO LESS *HELLISH.*

GRR!

〈RNGH!〉

AND, AS IN NATURE--

AAAIIEE!!

--*DEATH* MADE NO DISTINCTION.

85

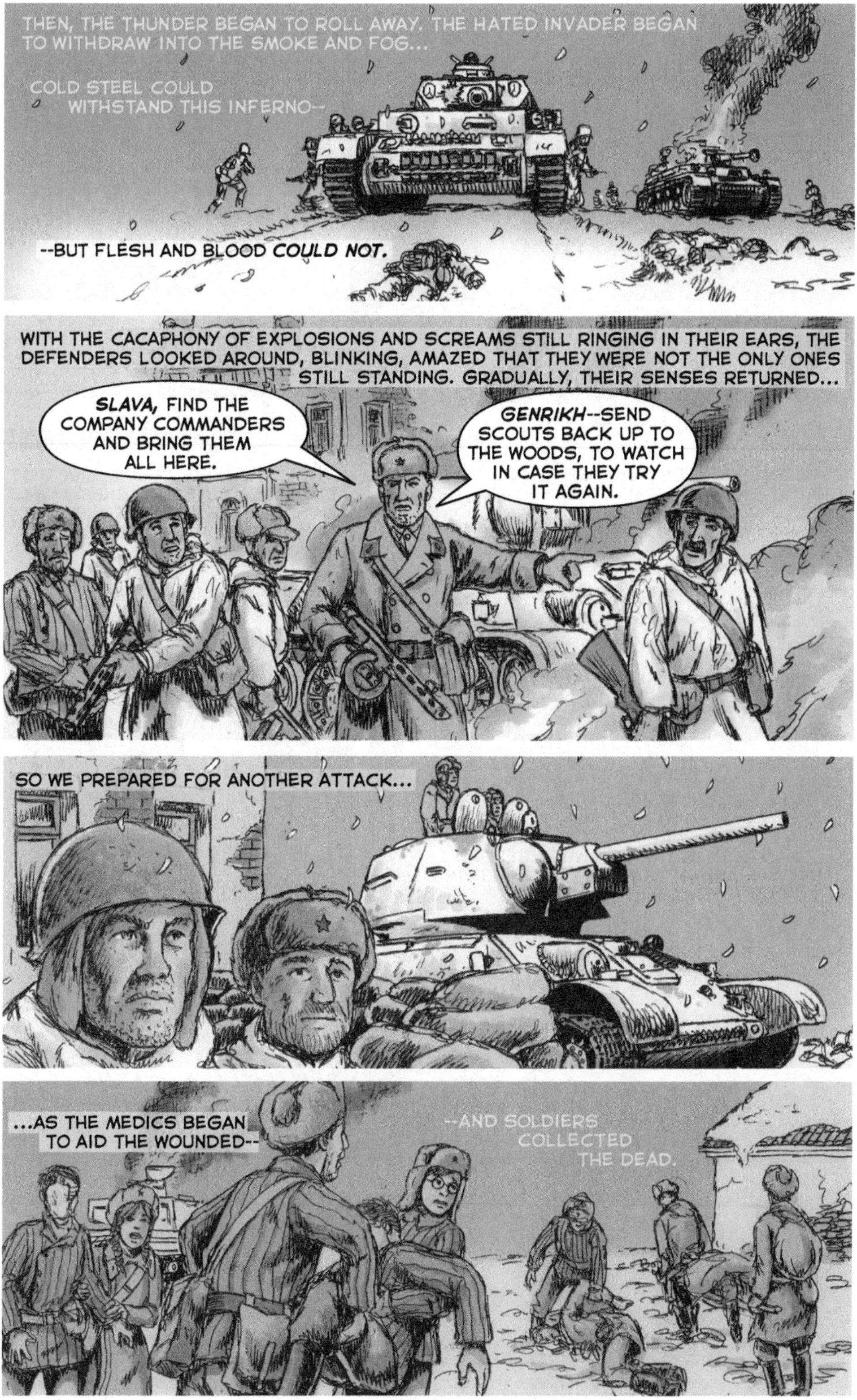
THEN, THE THUNDER BEGAN TO ROLL AWAY. THE HATED INVADER BEGAN TO WITHDRAW INTO THE SMOKE AND FOG...
COLD STEEL COULD WITHSTAND THIS INFERNO--
--BUT FLESH AND BLOOD COULD NOT.
WITH THE CACAPHONY OF EXPLOSIONS AND SCREAMS STILL RINGING IN THEIR EARS, THE DEFENDERS LOOKED AROUND, BLINKING, AMAZED THAT THEY WERE NOT THE ONLY ONES STILL STANDING. GRADUALLY, THEIR SENSES RETURNED...
SLAVA, FIND THE COMPANY COMMANDERS AND BRING THEM ALL HERE.
GENRIKH--SEND SCOUTS BACK UP TO THE WOODS, TO WATCH IN CASE THEY TRY IT AGAIN.
SO WE PREPARED FOR ANOTHER ATTACK...
...AS THE MEDICS BEGAN TO AID THE WOUNDED--
--AND SOLDIERS COLLECTED THE DEAD.

THEY BROUGHT THE WOUNDED TO THE KOLKHOZ'S* MEETING HALL. MANY HAD SUFFERED GHASTLY, LIFE-SHATTERING WOUNDS THAT WOULD SCAR THEM ALL THEIR LIVES--*IF* THEIR LIVES LASTED THAT LONG. THE MOST GREVIOUSLY INJURED ONES HELD SUCH TENUOUS HOLDS ON LIFE THAT THEIR PASSAGE TO THE OTHER SIDE WAS SCARCELY DETECTABLE.

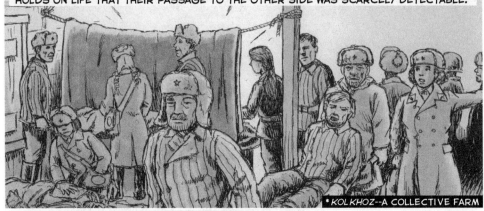

*KOLKHOZ--A COLLECTIVE FARM

I HELPED THE MEDICS AS BEST I COULD, WISHING I HAD SPENT MORE TIME LOOKING OVER THE SHOULDER OF MY NURSE-MOTHER... BUT MANY WERE BEYOND HELP.

I HAD BEEN AT IT FOR A WHILE BEFORE I BECAME AWARE THAT I HAD BEEN CRYING.

THEN I LOOKED UP--AND SAW THAT COMMISSAR STEPHAN CHEKOV WAS WATCHING ME INTENTLY. HIS COLD, BLACK EYES DID NOT BLINK ONCE.

HE CONTINUED TO STARE UNTIL I TURNED AWAY.

BUT--THE MOST SHOCKING EVENT OF THAT DAY WAS COLONEL NOZDRIN'S ASSESSMENT OF THE HUMAN COST OF THE BATTLE...

SO, WE LOST 12 TANKS AND 37 CREW MEMBERS...

...AND AS OF RIGHT NOW, THE TOTAL IS 17 INFANTRYMEN DEAD AND 42 WOUNDED.

SO, I'D SAY THAT WE HAVEN'T DONE BADLY AT *ALL*.

"...WE HAVEN'T DONE BADLY AT ALL!"

MANSTEIN'S OFFENSIVE SOON PETERED OUT, BUT NOT BECAUSE HE DIDN'T HAVE THE STRENGTH TO CONTINUE OR THE WILL TO DEMAND THE SACRIFICE--SUCCESS HAD ALL ALONG DEPENDED ON THE GERMAN **6TH ARMY** MOUNTING AN OFFENSIVE OF THEIR OWN TO BREAK OUT OF THE RING AT STALINGRAD. BUT THOSE GERMAN TROOPS MAROONED INSIDE STALINGRAD HADN'T ENOUGH FUEL FOR THEIR VEHICLES TO GO TWENTY MILES.

NOR DID THEY HAVE THE STRENGTH--
BECAUSE BY NOW THEY WERE **STARVING.**

BUT THE **MAIN** REASON THEY WERE TRAPPED WAS **HITLER**--HE WOULD NOT ALLOW THEM TO BREAK OUT. HIS ENORMOUS EGO MADE HIM REFUSE TO GIVE UP THE CITY AFTER HAVING INVESTED SO MUCH IN CAPTURING IT. IN THE END, THE GERMAN **6TH ARMY** SUCCUMBED NOT ONLY TO THE BLOWS OF THE RED ARMY OR BITTER WINDS OF THE RUSSIAN WINTER--
BUT TO THE SHORTSIGHTED TREACHERY OF THEIR **OWN LEADER.**

WHEN THE LAST GERMAN HOLDOUTS SURRENDERED ON **FEBRUARY 3, 1943,** THEY WERE BARELY RECOGNIZABLE AS THE STERLING PROFESSIONALS WHO'D ONCE TAKEN PARIS AND KIEV. THERE WERE ONLY **91,000** OF THEM LEFT, RAGGED AND STARVING...

LOOK, ALL OF YOU! LOOK!

THIS IS WHAT YOUR **BERLIN** WILL SOON LOOK LIKE!

IN THE NEXT FEW MONTHS, HALF OF THESE MEN WOULD DIE IN A TYPHUS EPIDEMIC. THE LAST OF THEM WOULD RETURN TO GERMANY IN **1955**--ONLY **6,000** STRONG.

WHEN THOSE FEW CIVILIAN SURVIVORS FINALLY CRAWLED FROM THE RUBBLE THAT HAD BEEN STALINGRAD, THEY FOUND THEIR CITY WAS A SMOKING RUIN, ITS SHATTERED STREETS CHOKED WITH SOME *200,000* CORPSES. BUT BESIDES THIS GRIM HARVEST, THEY DISCOVERED SOMETHING ELSE...

THEY NO LONGER REGARDED THOSE GERMANS WHOM THEY ONCE DREADED AND FEARED AS FORMIDABLE *SUPERMEN.*

THEY ALSO HAD BEGUN TO REALIZE THAT THE SOVIET UNION COULD WIN-- ALTHOUGH THE TIME REQUIRED AND THE PRICE TO BE PAID WERE YET UNDETERMINED.

WE HELD THE LINE AT *TWO CHURCHES* FOR A MONTH, BUT SAW NO FURTHER STRIFE. WE BURIED OUR DEAD, LUBED OUR TRACKS, CLEANED OUR GUNS, TUNED OUR ENGINES-- THEN RODE NORTH TO A RAILHEAD TO BE LOADED ONTO TRAINS AND SHIPPED WEST TO FOLLOW THE BATTLE.

COULD I PERHAPS RIDE UP TOP?

SURE!

THE COLONEL'S IN HIS *GAZ* WITH HIS DRIVER. BUT YOU'D BEST HANG ON--! MILLA AND I ARE IN A HURRY TO GET BACK TO *UKRAINE.*

I WAS JUST WATCHING COMMISSAR CHEKOV OVER THERE AT THE GRAVESITES...

IS THAT THE GRAVE OF A SOLDIER WHO WAS SOMEONE SPECIAL TO HIM?

HE WAS A PEASANT BOY FROM ULYANOVSK--STEPHAN WAS TEACHING HIM TO READ.

DURING THE ATTACK, THE BOY GOT SCARED AND TURNED TO RUN...

...SO STEPHAN SHOT HIM *DEAD*.

ANY FURTHER CONVERSATION BECAME IMPOSSIBLE AS OUR SQUEALING DIESEL ENGINES ROARED TO LIFE. THE COLONEL STOOD BESIDE HIS *GAZ* JEEP AND EYED HIS WARRIORS WITH PRIDE BEFORE HE WAVED HIS ARM AND SETTLED INTO HIS SEAT FOR A LONG MARCH.

OUR CLANKING, BANGING TANK TRACKS DISTURBED A HANDFUL OF SKINNY CHICKENS THAT HAD BEEN SEARCHING FOR ANY FORGOTTEN CRUMBS ON THE BARREN SOIL. THEY FLED AS WE GROUND DOWN THE BROWN-BLACK PATH, SLINGING NEW MUD INTO OLD. THE INFANTRYMEN RIDING ON THE BACKS OF THE *T-34*s GRABBED THE HANDRAILS TIGHTLY TO PREVENT BEING SLUNG OFF WHILE THEY ATTEMPTED TO GRAB SOME SMALL MEASURE OF ELUSIVE SLEEP.

I SLID DOWN INTO MY REGULAR SEAT BESIDE MILLA, AND AS SHE DROVE, I FOLDED MY ARMS UNDER MY SHEEPSKIN COAT AND TRIED TO STAVE OFF THE ICE-BOX COLD OF OUR TANK'S INTERIOR. I WEDGED MY SHOULDER AGAINST THE RADIO SET SO I COULD HALF-LISTEN TO THE SCRATCHY STATIC MUMBLING THAT PERHAPS COULD BE MY MASTER'S VOICE.

THE THROBBING OF THE ENGINE MUFFLED BY MY LEATHER HELMET WAS ENOUGH TO LULL ME TO SLEEP. I DRIFTED OFF INTO A SWEET SLUMBER, JUST AS IF I WERE A NAPPING CHILD ROCKED IN HER MOTHER'S ARMS.

Katusha

FEBRUARY, 1943. THE SOVIET WINTER OFFENSIVE WAS STILL ROLLING. RUSSIAN FORCES WERE BEATING AGAINST THE GERMANS OF *ARMY GROUP A,* WHO WERE TRYING DESPERATELY TO HOLD ONTO THE CITY OF *ROSTOV-ON-DON.* IF ROSTOV FELL, ALL THE GERMAN FORCES IN THE CAUCASUS WOULD BE CUT OFF.

OUR BRIGADE HAD REJOINED OUR CORPS, AND WE WERE ADVANCING ACROSS THE DONETS RIVER TOWARD *KHARKOV...*

MANY AMONG US WERE EXCITED TO BE RETURNING TO *UKRAINE.*

THE COLONEL WAS ABOUT TO GIVE THE COMMAND FOR OUR BRIGADE TO ADVANCE WHEN HE NOTICED A GROUP OF JOURNALISTS FROM THE ARMY PAPER *KRASNAYA ZVEZDA* (RED STAR) STANDING NEARBY. ONE OF THEM WAS THE RENOWNED POET AND WRITER *VASILY GROSSMAN*--SO THE COLONEL DECIDED TO TRY SOMETHING A LITTLE MORE DRAMATIC.

INTO THE LAIR OF THE **FASCIST BEAST**--!

--ADVANCE!!

TEE HEE!
HA HA! HA HA HA!!
>GIGGLE!<
HEE HEE HEE!
>SNORT<

VORONEZH AND KURSK WERE LIBERATED. IN MID-FEBRUARY, ROSTOV WAS TAKEN, BUT NOT BEFORE THE GERMANS HAD WITHDRAWN FROM THE CAUCASUS.

FOR THE MOST PART, THESE PRIZES WERE DEPOPULATED AND SHATTERED, THEIR POWER AND WATER SYSTEMS WRECKED.

IN EVERY CITY OR TOWN, SEARCHERS DISCOVERED SOME REMNANT OF THE POPULATION WHO STILL PERSEVERED.

COME OUT-- OR GET A *GRENADE* IN YOUR LAP--!

DON'T, PLEASE!

WE'RE COMING OUT--!

AT FIRST, THE SURVIVORS WERE FEARFUL--BUT EVEN THE POPULACE WHO'D BEEN PERSECUTED BY THE COMMUNISTS BECAME OVERWHELMED WITH JOY TO SEE THEIR SOLDIERS RETURN.

WE'RE *YOUR* PEOPLE!

AH! COME OUT INTO THE *SUN,* MOTHER! YOUR CITY IS *SAFE!*

IT WAS THESE CHILDREN OF THE WAR WHO RETAINED THE CLEAREST IMAGE OF THEIR SAVIORS: THE GRITTY SHUFFLE OF THEIR HEAVY BOOTS, AND THEIR DEEP VOICES, SPEAKING RUSSIAN WITHOUT FEAR...

YOU MEAN... THE *GERMANS* ARE--?

YES! ALL *GONE!*

WE CHASED THOSE *DEVILS* BACK TO HELL!

TO THEM, THESE RED ARMY SOLDIERS WERE HEROES OF A GREAT EPIC.

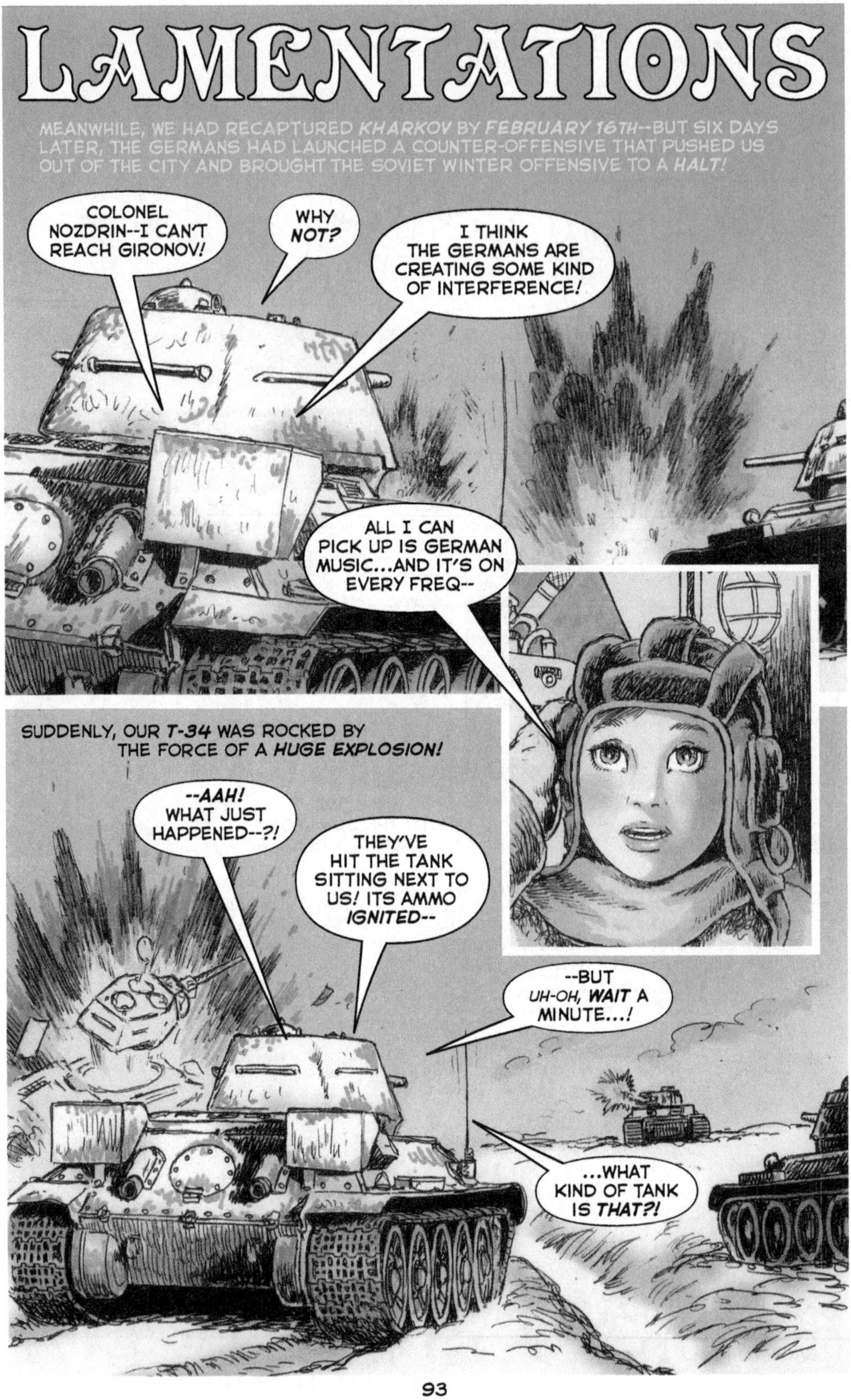
LAMENTATIONS
MEANWHILE, WE HAD RECAPTURED KHARKOV BY FEBRUARY 16TH--BUT SIX DAYS LATER, THE GERMANS HAD LAUNCHED A COUNTER-OFFENSIVE THAT PUSHED US OUT OF THE CITY AND BROUGHT THE SOVIET WINTER OFFENSIVE TO A HALT!
COLONEL NOZDRIN--I CAN'T REACH GIRONOV!
WHY NOT?
I THINK THE GERMANS ARE CREATING SOME KIND OF INTERFERENCE!
ALL I CAN PICK UP IS GERMAN MUSIC...AND IT'S ON EVERY FREQ--
SUDDENLY, OUR T-34 WAS ROCKED BY THE FORCE OF A HUGE EXPLOSION!
--AAH! WHAT JUST HAPPENED--?!
THEY'VE HIT THE TANK SITTING NEXT TO US! ITS AMMO IGNITED--
--BUT UH-OH, WAIT A MINUTE...!
...WHAT KIND OF TANK IS THAT?!

THE BIG GRAY-AND-WHITE BEAST SAT BOLDLY OUT IN THE OPEN, MAKING NO EFFORT TO HIDE ITS PRESENCE OR SEEK ADDITIONAL PROTECTION.

THIS WAS THE FIRST TIME OUR CREW HAD EVER SEEN A *TIGER TANK*, BUT IT ALSO MARKED ANOTHER FIRST FOR US--

--BEING *HIT* BY ONE!

THE SHELL STRUCK THE FRONT OF OUR LEFT TRACK, SHATTERING IT AND TAKING OUT ALL FIVE ROAD WHEELS--IN SHORT, EFFECTIVELY CRIPPLING OUR TANK'S MOVEMENT/ THERE WOULD BE NO MORE ADVANCING FOR *US*...

BUT NOT SO FOR ANOTHER OF OUR *T-34*s. JUST THEN, IT ROARED BY ON OUR RIGHT SIDE--HEADING STRAIGHT AT THE *TIGER!*

IT WAS FIRING ON THE MOVE, ITS SHOTS GOING WILD...BUT THE BRAVERY OF OUR COMRADES-IN-ARMS BOUGHT US THE VALUABLE TIME THAT MILLA NEEDED. USING ONLY THE RIGHT TRACK...

...SHE MANAGED TO STEER US OVER A SHALLOW DITCH!

EVERYONE OUT THE FLOOR HATCH!

I HAD ALWAYS SAID MY SISTER COULD GET THE MOST OUT OF THE LEAST--BUT I'D HAD *NO IDEA.*

THE T-34 THAT HAD PASSED US WAS UNDER THE COMMAND OF YAKOV PETESKY, A YOUNG SERGEANT FROM NOVGOROD WHO'D ALWAYS HAD A REPUTATION FOR RECKLESSNESS. YAKOV'S NOBLE SACRIFICE GAVE US ENOUGH TIME TO GET OUT OF OUR TANK, SLIP DOWN INTO THE DITCH, AND MAKE A RUN FOR IT.

BUT MISHA BOVA'S YEAR-OLD LEG WOUND HADN'T PROPERLY HEALED, AND HE HAD A HARD TIME KEEPING UP. COLONEL NOZDRIN AND I HELPED HIM ALONG...

...BUT THE EVER-PRACTICAL MILLA BECAME IMPATIENT WITH OUR SLOW PACE.

HERE--TAKE THE *GUN*, KATUSHA. IF I HELP, WE CAN MOVE FASTER!

WE HAD SCARCELY GONE A HUNDRED YARDS-- BEFORE I FOUND A PERFECT USE FOR IT.

I WAS THANKFUL THE AWFUL NOISE OF THE BATTLE HELPED MASK ANY SOUND OF OUR APPROACH...

⦂YAAGGH!⦂

JUST BECAUSE I COULD *DO* IT *DIDN'T* MEAN THAT I WAS *USED* TO IT.

I KNELT TO COLLECT THE AMMO FROM THE BODIES--BUT WHEN I FOUND THAT THEY HAD NONE LEFT ON THEM, I LET OUT A CURSE THAT WAS WORTHY OF COLONEL NOZDRIN HIMSELF.

I STOOD THERE A MOMENT, SHOCKED AT MYSELF...AND THEN I RACED TO CATCH UP WITH THE OTHERS.

MEANWHILE, OUR BRIGADE HAD LOST MANY TANKS, AND THE INFANTRY HAD SUSTAINED HEAVY CASUALTIES. THEY'D BEEN FORCED BACK, BUT MANAGED TO WEAVE THEMSELVES INTO A STRONG LINE HELD BY A VETERAN RIFLE DIVISION FRESH FROM THE CONFLICT AT *STALINGRAD*. AS THE BATTLE RAGED, THEY TRIED TO ASSESS THE SITUATION...

GUCHKOV'S BATTALION LOST THE LEAST--HE STILL HAS ELEVEN TANKS...

DID ANYONE HAPPEN TO SEE WHAT BECAME OF *COLONEL NOZDRIN'S* TANK?

I SAW ONE OF THOSE *TIGERS* BLOW HIS TRACK OFF!

NO--! DID YOU SEE IF THEY BAILED OUT? AND DID THEY *ALL* GET AWAY?

I BELIEVE SO, CAPTAIN KOVCHENKO...

I SAW FOUR PEOPLE RUN DOWN THAT LONG DITCH THAT CUTS ACROSS THE PLAIN...

IT LOOKED LIKE IT WAS THE *COLONEL*, HIS GUNNER *BOVA*--

--AND BOTH OF THE *TYMOSHENKO* SISTERS.

WHICH DIRECTION DID THEY GO?

WE HEADED EAST ACROSS A STRANGELY FAMILIAR LANDSCAPE. WE TRIED TO LIE LOW DURING THE DAY AND ONLY MOVE BY NIGHT, BECAUSE THE AREA WAS PRACTICALLY CRAWLING WITH GERMAN PATROLS. OUR LUCK RAN OUT ON THE MORNING OF THE THIRD DAY-- WE GOT CAUGHT OUT IN THE OPEN BEFORE WE HAD THE CHANCE TO REACH A HIDING PLACE.

ALL RIGHT, IVAN! COME OUT OF YOUR HOLE!

WE'VE ONLY GOT 18 ROUNDS FOR THE PAPASHAW--AND ONE CLIP EACH FOR OUR TWO PISTOLS...

THAT'S NOT MUCH AGAINST A 20MM...

IT DOESN'T MATTER--I'M NOT GOING TO SURRENDER!

...BUT SOMEONE ELSE HAD A MUCH DIFFERENT OUTCOME IN MIND!

COME ON, YOU RUSSIAN SCUM--!

IT LOOKED LIKE IT WAS ALL OVER FOR US...

COME OUT, OR ELSE I START SHOOTING!

ON THE COUNT OF THREE--

--THAT IS, IF YOU IDIOTS CAN COUNT THAT HIGH, HAHA!

YOU KNOW--LIKE ONE...

TWO...

BUT IT TURNED OUT THAT HE COULDN'T COUNT THAT HIGH.

97

HAVE YOU TWO FORGOTTEN *EVERYTHING* I TAUGHT YOU?

:GASP!:

AAH!!

HAHAHA!

WE PASSED A BEAT-UP LITTLE TOWN ON OUR WAY HERE. WE'LL HOLE UP THERE UNTIL WE SEE WHICH WAY THE WIND IS BLOWING...

WHATEVER YOU SAY, UNCLE TARAS!

NOW WAIT A MINUTE! I SHOULD HAVE SOMETHING TO SAY ABOUT THIS--!

...AND WHO IN *HELL* ARE YOU...?

I AM *LIEUTENANT COLONEL RUSLAW NOZDRIN*--!

--AND THESE SOLDIERS ARE UNDER *MY* COMMAND!

WELL, HOW LUCKY FOR YOU. SINCE I'M TAKING THEM TO SAFETY, I'LL ALLOW YOU TO TAG ALONG...

...*OR* YOU CAN STAY *HERE*. IT HARDLY MATTERS TO ME.

I TOOK OVER HELPING MISHA SO THAT MILLA COULD WALK ALONG AHEAD OF US WITH UNCLE TARAS. I COULD HEAR THE COLONEL GRUMBLING UNDER HIS BREATH-- BUT HE DIDN'T KEEP IT UP FOR VERY LONG.

I'M AFRAID THAT THE CHURCH IS QUITE TORN UP, TOO. BUT SEE THAT *SMOKE* RISING UP OVER THERE...?

WHOEVER THEY ARE, I JUST HOPE THEY'RE FRIENDLIES...

UNCLE TARAS TOLD US ABOUT HIS TWO COMPANIONS...

"ANATOLY WAS IN PRISON FOR PETTY THIEVERY. THEY LET HIM OUT TO JOIN THE ARMY...

"BATAAR IS A KALMYK WHO'D BEEN FALSELY ARRESTED AS A COLLABORATOR. I TALKED THE *NKVD* INTO RELEASING HIM..."

I COULD JUST IMAGINE *HOW* UNCLE TARAS DID *THAT...!*

ALL WE FOUND IN THE CHURCH WAS AN OLD, SICK PRIEST AND A FEW OLD WOMEN WHO WERE TAKING CARE OF HIM.

BATAAR, WHY DON'T YOU FIND THE HIGHEST WINDOW AND KEEP AN EYE OUT...

UNCLE TARAS, THIS LADY COULD USE OUR HELP.

WE MUST HAVE A *FUNERAL* THIS AFTERNOON. IT IS THE THIRD DAY...

WE TRIED TO DIG THE GRAVE, BUT WE COULD NOT--THE GROUND IS FAR TOO *FROZEN!*

I THINK WE CAN DO THAT, SISTER-- WE'LL BE *HAPPY* TO HELP YOU GOOD LADIES OUT.

COLONEL NOZDRIN--SINCE YOU ARE NO DOUBT A PARTY MAN, AND AS SUCH ARE UNFAMILIAR WITH THE RITUALS OF THE ORTHODOX CHURCH...

...WHY DON'T YOU GO UPSTAIRS AND KEEP WATCH WITH OUR BUDDHIST FRIEND?

UNCLE TARAS LOOSENED UP THE FROZEN SOIL USING A COUPLE OF GRENADES...

THERE! NOW, LET'S DIG OUT THE LOOSE DIRT.

UNCLE TARAS--? I REALLY WISH THAT YOU WOULDN'T ANTAGONIZE COLONEL NOZDRIN...

HE TRULY *IS* A VERY GOOD COMMANDING OFFICER...

I *KNOW* THAT, KATUSHA-- I COULD IMMEDIATELY TELL HE WAS. I SIMPLY WANTED TO IMPRESS ON HIM THE GREAT *IMPORTANCE* OF TAKING THE BEST CARE OF YOU AND MILLA...

BUT *DON'T* FRET. I'LL BE SURE TO INCLUDE HIM IN ALL OUR IMPORTANT SURVIVAL DECISIONS...

...LIKE WHERE TO DIG A *LATRINE.*

THAT AFTERNOON, THEY BROUGHT OUT THE BODY OF THE MAN WHO WAS TO BE BURIED. APPARENTLY THE LAST MALE LEFT IN TOWN AFTER THE PRIEST. HE WAS VERY OLD-- IN HIS LONG LIFE, HE'D HAD TWO WIVES, ALONG WITH MANY CHILDREN AND GRANDCHILDREN...BUT HE HAD OUTLIVED MOST OF THEM.

COLONEL NOZDRIN, TOO, CAME OUT WITH US. BUT HE SEEMED A BIT UNCOMFORTABLE AND OUT OF PLACE, GIVEN THE CIRCUMSTANCES.

JUST AS THE PRIEST BEGAN TO SPEAK, AN OLD WOMAN WRAPPED IN A BLACK SHAWL BEGAN TO WAIL AND WRING HER HANDS. SHE FLUNG HERSELF ONTO THE SNOW, CRYING OUT LIKE ALL THE DEATH OF THE WORLD WERE PUSHING HER DOWN.

I COULD TELL THAT THE COLONEL WAS UNNERVED BY HER DISPLAY...

...AND THEN THE OTHER WOMEN JOINED HER.

JUST WHAT IS *WRONG* WITH THESE WOMEN?

THEY ARE *MOURNING,* COLONEL.

UNCLE TARAS FIXED HIM WITH A GLARE AS SHARP AS A PAIR OF KNIVES.

THIS IS ABOUT *LOSS.* IT'S WHAT THEY DO WHEN THEY LOSE A HUSBAND OR SON OR DAUGHTER. THEY BELIEVE THIS MAN'S GOING TO A BETTER PLACE.

BUT THEY MOURN HIS DEPARTURE, AND FOR THE HARD LIFE HE'S LIVED.

THE PRIEST WENT ON, NOT AT ALL BOTHERED BY THE WOMEN'S UNEARTHLY POETRY OF LAMENT.

WITH THE SAINTS, LET THE SOUL OF THY SERVANT GO IN PEACE, O CHRIST, WHERE THERE IS NEITHER PAIN NOR SORROW NOR LAMENTATION, BUT ETERNAL LIFE...

WHEN I WAS LITTLE, I ONCE QUESTIONED MY MOTHER ABOUT THE SAME THING--WHY DO THESE WOMEN PROJECT SUCH AGONY AND PAIN?

SHE TOLD ME THAT WE CANNOT KNOW. WE UNDERSTAND NEITHER WHAT THESE WOMEN HAVE LIVED THROUGH, NOR THE HARDSHIPS THAT THEY HAVE EXPERIENCED.

SHE SAID THAT ONE DAY, WHEN I WAS OLDER, I WOULD UNDERSTAND. AND THEN SHE SAID--

--"NEVER JUDGE SOMEONE ELSE'S JOYS OR SORROWS."

SO, COLONEL--I IMAGINE ALL THAT WAS PROBABLY A NEW EXPERIENCE FOR YOU...

WELL, COMRADE TYMOSHENKO...

AS A COMMUNIST, I *AM*, OF COURSE, AN *ATHEIST*--

--BUT... NOT SO VERY *STRONGLY*.

THAT EVENING, SOME OF THE VILLAGE WOMEN CAME TO THE CHURCH WITH FOOD FOR US. IT WAS OBVIOUS THEY HAD BUT LITTLE...BUT WE WERE HUNGRY AND GRATEFUL.

UNCLE TARAS HAD NOTICED THE LOOKS MISHA BOVA GAVE MILLA.

I SEE THAT BOY HAS A THING FOR YOU...

WELL, TOO BAD FOR HIM--HE CAN *KEEP* IT.

HAS IT BEEN VERY BAD HERE UNDER THE GERMANS?

OH, YES! THEY WERE JUST LIKE THE *CHEKA* WERE, LONG AGO...!

...THEY KIDNAPPED OUR YOUNG ONES FOR SLAVE LABOR, OR KILLED WHOEVER THEY WISHED.

WE HAD HOPED THEY'D DISSOLVE THE *KOLKHOZES*. BUT THEY DECIDED TO USE THE SYSTEM FOR THEIR OWN BENEFIT--

BUT *WHY* WOULD YOU WANT THEM TO DISSOLVE THE *KOLKHOZES*? THAT IS A GREAT SYSTEM!

COLLECTIVE FARMS BROUGHT *SOCIALISM* TO THE COUNTRYSIDE!

EVERY EYE IN THE ROOM TURNED TO LOOK AT COLONEL NOZDRIN,

YOU'RE FROM THE CITY, AREN'T YOU?

FROM MOSCOW, AS WERE MY FATHER AND GRANDFATHER BEFORE ME.

ALL RIGHT. LET'S SAY YOUR GRANDFATHER WORKED ALL HIS LIFE BUILDING AND GROWING A LITTLE SHOP TO SUPPORT HIS FAMILY. HE PASSED THE SHOP DOWN TO YOUR FATHER AND HE PASSED IT DOWN TO YOU. THIS WAS YOUR LIFE'S WORK, HOW YOU FED YOUR WIFE AND CHILDREN...

THEN ONE DAY SOME MEN CAME, AND THEY TOLD YOU THAT YOU NO LONGER OWNED THE SHOP, OR ANYTHING IN IT..

...THAT IT WAS BEING TAKEN AWAY "FOR THE STATE", FOR THE "GOOD OF THE PEOPLE"...

...AND IN THE PROCESS, ALL THE FOOD WAS TAKEN FROM YOU, AND EVERY VESTIGE OF YOUR ABILITY TO PROTECT AND FEED YOUR FAMILY.

BUT, COLLECTIVIZATION *WAS* FOR THE GOOD OF THE PEOPLE. IT WAS ESTABLISHED TO DESTROY CAPITALISM, AND ESTABLISH SOCIALISM IN THE COUNTRYSIDE...

...IT WAS ALSO TO GET RID OF THE WORST OFFENDEDS OF THE CAPITALIST, THE *KULAKS!*

COLLECTIVIZATION ALLOWED US TO ILLIMINATE THE *KULAKS* AS A CLASS.

104

BUT AT THAT, MILLA EXPLODED IN *RAGE!*

WHO WERE THE KULAKS? YOU HAVE NO IDEA--! THE "RICH PEASANTS," YOU CALL THEM...?!!

MY FAMILY WAS *NOT* RICH--YET MY OWN FATHER WAS *CONDEMNED* BY YOUR GLORIOUS *SOCIALIST STATE--!*

WHA--?

AND *WHY--?*

--BECAUSE HE WORKED HARD! HE MANAGED TO PUT A TIN ROOF ON OUR TINY HOUSE, WOODEN PLANKS OVER THE DIRT FLOOR...AND JUST BECAUSE WE HAD A LITTLE MORE THAN OTHERS HAD--

--MY FATHER WAS *ARRESTED,* THEN *SHOT...*AS A *"KULAK"!*

"THE *HELL* THEY VISITED ON US IS *SEARED* INTO MY MEMORY...

"I REMEMBER HOW THE *'REQUISITION SQUADS'* CAME TO OUR TOWN AND TOOK *EVERYTHING* THE PEOPLE HAD, EVERY LAST GRAIN OF WHEAT! THEY LEFT MY MOTHER, MY TWO LITTLE SISTERS, AND ME WITH NOTHING--*NOTHING!*

"THEY LEFT US TO STARVE...

"...AND STARVE, WE *DID.* MY BABY SISTER DIED FIRST. MY MOTHER HAD NO CHOICE--TO KEEP US ALIVE...SHE FED US OUR *SISTER'S FLESH.*

"BUT THAT DIDN'T LAST. MY OTHER SISTER DIED--AND MY MOTHER JUST LOST HER MIND FROM *DESPAIR.*

"SO...MAMA *HANGED HERSELF.*

"I WAS LEFT ALONE WITH HER. AND FOR DAYS, I SURVIVED, ONLY BY-- BY LIVING OFF--OHH, GOD--!!"

"I CAN'T RECALL LEAVING. ALL OF A SUDDEN, I WAS OUT WANDERING IN THE SNOW, FREEZING..."

"IF KATUSHA'S FATHER HADN'T FOUND ME DIGGING IN THE GARBAGE TO FIND FOOD, I SURELY WOULD HAVE *DIED*.

"OR EVEN *WORSE*--I WOULD HAVE GONE ON LIVING AS I HAD..."

MILLA STOPPED SPEAKING, AND SILENCE FELL UPON US LIKE A PALL. SHE STOOD THERE FOR A MOMENT, IN MUTE AGONY...

...THEN SHE TURNED AND WALKED OUT OF THE ROOM.

IT SEEMED LIKE AN ETERNITY PASSED BEFORE WE COULD SPEAK AGAIN.

KATUSHA...HAS MILLA EVER TOLD YOU OF THIS BEFORE--?

NO, NOT A WORD! I'VE *NEVER* HEARD ANY OF THIS BEFORE JUST NOW...!

UNCLE TARAS GOT UP AND FOLLOWED MILLA.

THAT NIGHT, I DIDN'T SLEEP WELL. I DON'T THINK ANY OF US DID.

I KNOW COLONEL NOZDRIN *DIDN'T*.

106

I HAD NO TROUBLE GETTING UP FOR THE LAST WATCH UPSTAIRS.

IT WAS ABOUT TWO HOURS FROM SUNRISE WHEN I SPOTTED THEM...

UH-OH!

UNCLE TARAS! GET UP HERE... QUICK!

EH--?

LIGHTS! COMING FROM THE WEST!

OKAY! GET EVERYBODY UP AND MOVING!

THERE IS A STONE BARN DOWN BY THE STREAM THAT WOULD BE A GOOD PLACE TO HIDE OUT...

BATAAR! YOU AND ANATOLY FIND A SAFE PLACE TO WATCH THEM, THEN COME REPORT TO ME.

WE DID OUR BEST AT ERASING ANY EVIDENCE THAT WE HAD BEEN IN THE CHURCH, THEN WE HEADED DOWN TO THE BARN. FROM THERE, WE WOULD DECIDE WHAT OUR OPTIONS WERE.

THERE'S ONE SMALL HALF-TRACK WITH FIVE MEN AND A MACHINE GUN, THEN TWO BIG HALF-TRACKS WITH SIX MEN EACH. WE ALSO SAW TWO *88MM* FIELD GUNS, AND WHAT LOOKS LIKE PLENTY OF AMMO.

WELL--THERE IS STILL ENOUGH DARK TO SLIP OFF TO THE EAST...

BUT--

"BUT" *WHAT,* COLONEL?

THOSE TWO 88'S ALONE COULD TAKE OUT *DOZENS* OF OUR TANKS IF THEY CAUGHT THEM CROSSING THE OPEN GROUND TO THE EAST...!

WE *MUST* DO SOMETHING TO DISABLE THEM!

UNCLE TARAS RELUCTANTLY AGREED WITH THE COLONEL TO RECONNOITER THE SITUATION BEFORE COMMITTING TO ANY ACTION. TO HIS CREDIT, THE COLONEL DIDN'T TRY "PULLING RANK" ON HIM--HE AGREED TO ABIDE BY TARAS'S DECISION.

OKAY...

"THE GUNS ARE ON THE EDGE OF TOWN. THESE ARTILLERY MEN ARE PROBABLY NOT READY TO DEAL WITH A SMALL, SWIFT ATTACK.

"THE TWO MEN IN THE CHURCH WITH A PHONE LINE STRUNG TO THE GUNS ARE NO DOUBT ARTILLERY OBSERVERS.

"THREE MEN ON A MACHINE GUN WILL BE COVERING THE ARTILLERY'S RIGHT FLANK-- WE WILL HAVE TO TAKE THEM OUT FOR SURE.

"AT LEAST THERE'S A STRONG WIND TONIGHT. IT WILL HELP COVER UP OUR MOVEMENTS..."

BETWEEN US, WE HAVE FOUR PISTOLS, FOUR *PPSH*'S, AND SIX GRENADES. I'D RATHER WE HAD MORE. PERHAPS YOU GIRLS SHOULD STAY HERE--

NO! WE WILL DO OUR PART, AS WE ALWAYS HAVE!

I HAD EXPECTED NO LESS OF YOU. ALL RIGHT--

HERE'S HOW WE'RE GOING TO DO IT...

WITH THE UTMOST STEALTH, MISHA, MILLA, AND I CREPT UP TO A POSITION NEAR THE MACHINE-GUN NEST AND WAITED...

ON THE STREET BEHIND THE GERMAN GUNS, BATAAR AND ANATOLY TOOK POSITION TO DELIVER THE MOST FIRE ON THEM WHEN THE RIGHT TIME CAME...

BUT AS UNCLE TARAS QUIETLY APPROACHED THE DOOR OF THE CHURCH WITH NOZDRIN, THE COLONEL PAUSED TO WHISPER...

TARAS, WAIT...I WANT TO ASK YOU A QUESTION.

AND WHAT IS THAT?

WHEN YOU LEFT YOUR UNIT TO LOOK FOR YOUR GIRLS--

--WHAT DID YOU TELL YOUR SUPERIORS?

I FIGHT *FIRST* FOR THOSE THINGS THAT I CARE ABOUT-- STALIN AND THE MOTHERLAND ARE WAY ON DOWN THE LIST. BATAAR AND ANATOLY CAME ALONG BECAUSE THEY OWE *ME*---NOT THE STATE.

EH--? I TOLD THEM *NOTHING!*

WELL...I CAN'T *APPROVE* OF WHAT YOU DID--

--BUT ALL THE SAME, I AM *GLAD* THAT YOU DID IT.

THEY SLIPPED IN AS QUIET AS THE CHURCH'S MICE. UNCLE TARAS SET ABOUT WORKING ON THE GERMAN OBSERVERS' PHONE CORD WITH HIS KNIFE--

--SLITTING IT HALFWAY THROUGH.

HELLO... *HELLO--! BLAST IT!*

THE COMMUNICATION WITH THE GUNS KEEPS BREAKING UP! CHECK THE LINE FOR A SHORT.

WELL, CHECK IT *AGAIN!*

BUT-- I *ALREADY* CHECKED IT!

"CHECK IT AGAIN," HE SAYS...

...BUT I ALREADY *DID*--!

GRUMBLE OH...WAIT--!

...A-HA! THERE IT IS--!

...*GRROOOHH*

HERE, COLONEL--HELP ME GET INTO HIS SNOW SUIT.

DID YOU FIND THE PROBLEM?

IT'S ON *YOUR* END.

WHA--?

⋅⋅AAAG--⋅⋅

⋅⋅--MMRF⋅⋅

THE COLONEL DONNED THE OTHER SNOW SUIT, AND THEY LOADED ON THE GERMANS' EQUIPMENT...

THIS SHOULD EVEN THINGS UP, *EH?*

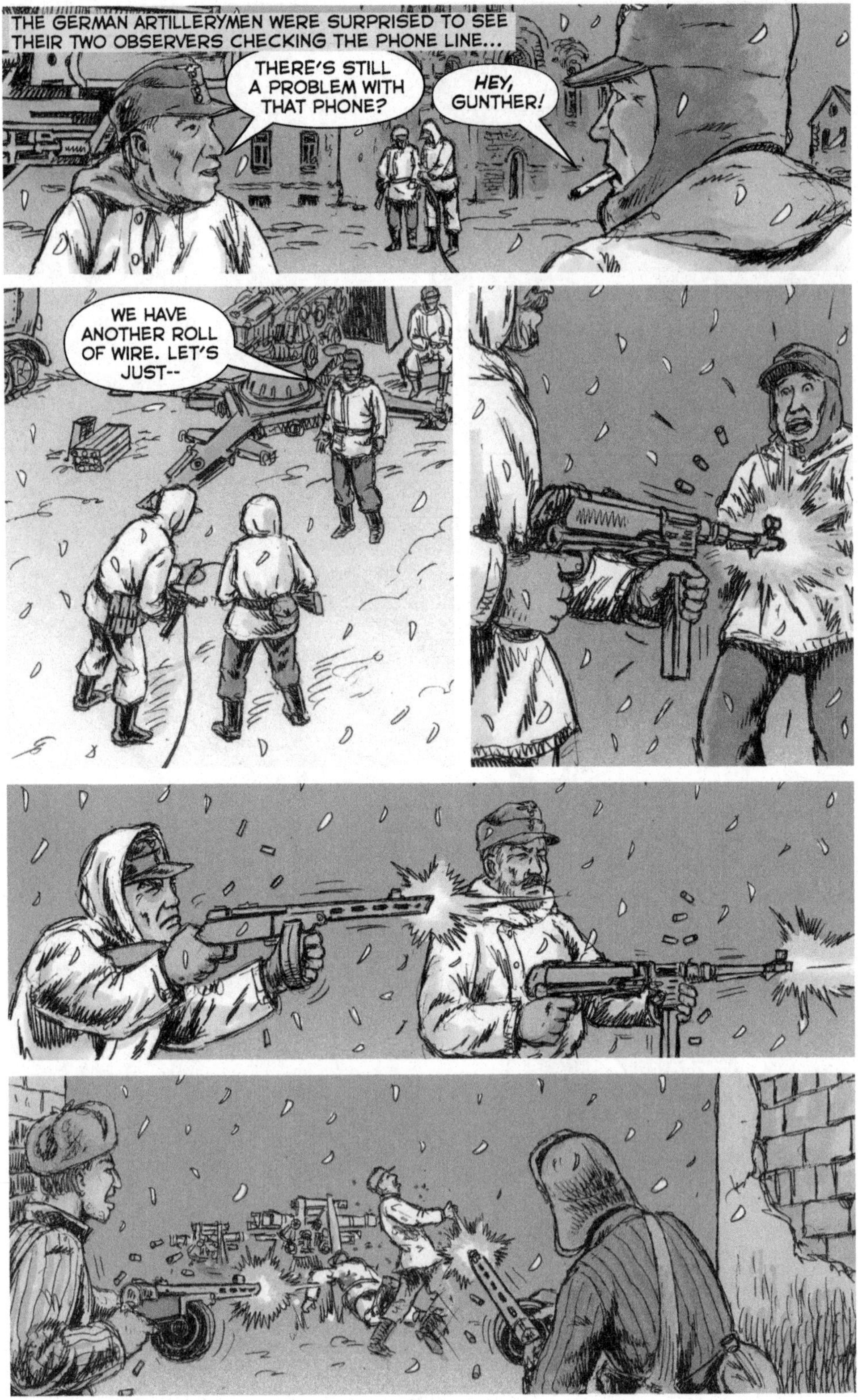
THE GERMAN ARTILLERYMEN WERE SURPRISED TO SEE THEIR TWO OBSERVERS CHECKING THE PHONE LINE...
THERE'S STILL A PROBLEM WITH THAT PHONE?
HEY, GUNTHER!
WE HAVE ANOTHER ROLL OF WIRE. LET'S JUST--

THAT'S OUR SIGNAL!

PULL AND THROW!

FIND ANY *WEAPONS* YOU CAN-- THEN LET'S GO HELP THE OTHERS!

MANY OF THE ARTILLERYMEN WERE CAUGHT OUT IN THE OPEN AND KILLED--BUT OTHERS GRABBED WEAPONS AND TOOK COVER AROUND THEIR GUNS!

LET'S MOVE TO THE LEFT TO TRY TO GET BEHIND 'EM!

SEEING UNCLE TARAS AND THE COLONEL MOVING GAVE TWO GERMANS THE IDEA TO TRY A SIMILAR MANEUVER...

...BUT THEY RAN RIGHT INTO *MILLA!*

IT HAS ALWAYS AMAZED ME HOW SO MANY PEOPLE LACK BOTH IMAGINATION AND COMMON SENSE. A PERFECT EXAMPLE WAS THE GERMAN WHO DECIDED TO CLIMB ATOP HIS OWN AMMO-LADEN HALF-TRACK IN ORDER TO THROW A GRENADE...!

THE GRENADE FELL IN AMONG THE BOXES OF *88MM* AMMO-- RIGHT BETWEEN TWO CANS OF GASOLINE AND A TELLER MINE!

UNCLE TARAS SAW IT LAND--BUT COLONEL NOZDRIN, DISTRACTED BY THE GUNFIRE, DIDN'T NOTICE IT!

OH, NO--!!

EH--?

--RUN!

WHAT DID YOU-- ⌇ERK!⌇

RUN!!

THE HORRIFIC BLAST EFFECTIVELY PUT AN END TO THE FIGHT AS THE GERMAN ARTILLERYMEN WERE PULVERIZED OR SHREDDED WHEREVER THEY STOOD...

...AND A HUGE *FIREBALL* LIT UP THE PRE-DAWN SKIES!

⸫GASP⸫ GOD...!

UNCLE TARAS AND COLONEL NOZDRIN LAY SPRAWLED ON THE GROUND, NICKED AND BLEEDING, THEIR GERMAN SNOW SUITS PRACTICALLY RIPPED FROM THEIR BODIES...

⸫UHHN...⸫

...BUT THEY WERE *ALIVE!*

THEN UNCLE TARAS FLASHED HIS BIG SMILE AT MILLA...

...AND MILLA SMILED BACK.

THEN UNCLE TARAS ROSE--BUT HIS MOTIONS WERE SHAKY, HIS LEGS WOBBLING UNDER HIM...

...HE DROPPED HIS WEAPON...

THE LOOK ON HIS FACE WAS ONE I HAD NEVER SEEN BEFORE--AND TO THIS DAY, ONE THAT I CANNOT FULLY UNDERSTAND.

THEN, BEFORE WE COULD REACH HIM--HE FELL BACK, ONTO THE HARD, COLD SNOW.

WE SAW HIS RIGHT SIDE WAS RIDDLED WITH SHRAPNEL AND SEEPING BLOOD. HE LET OUT A WEAK CHUCKLE...

HEH... CHEWED-- ;KOFF; --BY WOLVES...

PANTING WITH OUR DESPERATION, WE ALL GATHERED CLOSE AROUND HIM AS WE TRIED TO DETERMINE WHAT TO DO...

...WHEN THERE WAS NOTHING AT ALL THAT WE *COULD* DO.

AT THIS POINT, HIS FACE WAS JUST BARELY MOBILE--BUT HE DID MANAGE TO CAST ONE MEANINGFUL GLANCE AT COLONEL NOZDRIN.

A FAINT, FLEETING SMILE CROSSED MY UNCLE'S LIPS...

MILLA HOVERED OVER HIM, NOT BLINKING, NOT BREATHING, AS HER WHOLE LIFE HUNG BY SOMEONE ELSE'S THREAD...

THEN...LIKE THE ESCAPING OF SOME INSUBSTANTIAL VAPOR...

...TARAS TYMOSHENKO WAS *GONE*.

AS WE REMAINED THERE IN STUNNED SILENCE, A THIN VEIL OF PINK WASHED OVER US FROM THE EASTERN SKY. THE ONLY SOUNDS WERE THE CRACKLING OF FIRES AND THE WHISPER OF THE FRIGID WIND.

THE OLD WOMEN OF THE VILLAGE, FORGOTTEN IN THE HEAT OF BATTLE, NOW CAME FORTH FROM THEIR HOMES.

THEN--MILLA ROCKED BACK ON HER HEELS, ROLLED HER EYES TO THE SKY, AND LET OUT A SHRILL CRY OF ANGUISH THAT CUT US ALL TO THE CORE.

HER LONG SHRIEKS BROKE ONLY LONG ENOUGH FOR HER TO SUCK IN MORE OF THE COLD AIR TO FUEL ANOTHER HEART-RENDING HOWL OF PAIN.

I FELT MY CHEST QUAKE AND FLUTTER UNCONTROLLABLY AS MY TEARS WETTED THE FRONT OF HIS *TELOGREIKA* JACKET.

THE WOMEN OF THE VILLAGE FELL TO THE GROUND BESIDE US, THEIR WAILING LAMENTS FILLING THE ICY AIR LIKE SOME ANCIENT, PRIMAL SONG.

THE MEN STOOD BY IN AWKWARD HELPLESSNESS, THEIR FACES TIGHTENING INTO MARBLE AS THEY GRIPPED HARD ON THEIR WEAPONS, THEIR TEETH BARING CURSES AND OATHS.

UNCLE TARAS HAD ALWAYS SO VALUED THE GUIDANCE OF HIS OLD MENTOR, *SEMEN KALASHNIKOV*...WAS HE LISTENING TO HIS VOICE NOW? I REMEMBERED THE WAY UNCLE TARAS HAD STOOD OVER SEMEN'S GRAVE IN KROVROT, LISTENING SO INTENTLY...WHEN ALL *I* COULD HEAR WAS THE WIND.

BUT ALL I KNEW WAS ANOTHER PRECIOUS HUMAN VOICE HAD BEEN FOREVER SILENCED...

...BUT NOT THE WIND...

Katusha

SPRING, 1943... ALL ALONG THE 1,750-MILE FRONT THAT STRETCHED FROM LENINGRAD TO NOVOROSSIYSK, THE SNOW WAS FINALLY MELTING.

THE SPROUTING BUDS OF 1943 WERE VERY MUCH LIKE THOSE OF THE SPRING OF 1942: HARD, DARK, AND RUSTING, GIVING NO GREAT PROMISE OF A HARDY PLANTING SEASON WITH A BOUNTIFUL HARVEST TO COME.

BUT THIS YEAR, *MOTHER RUSSIA* WOULD YIELD A RICH HARVEST OF ANOTHER KIND...

...A HARVEST OF *CORRUPTION.*

A HARVEST FIT TO FEED THE CROWS AND THE SCAVENGERS...

...AND ONLY *GOD* KNOWS WHAT ELSE.

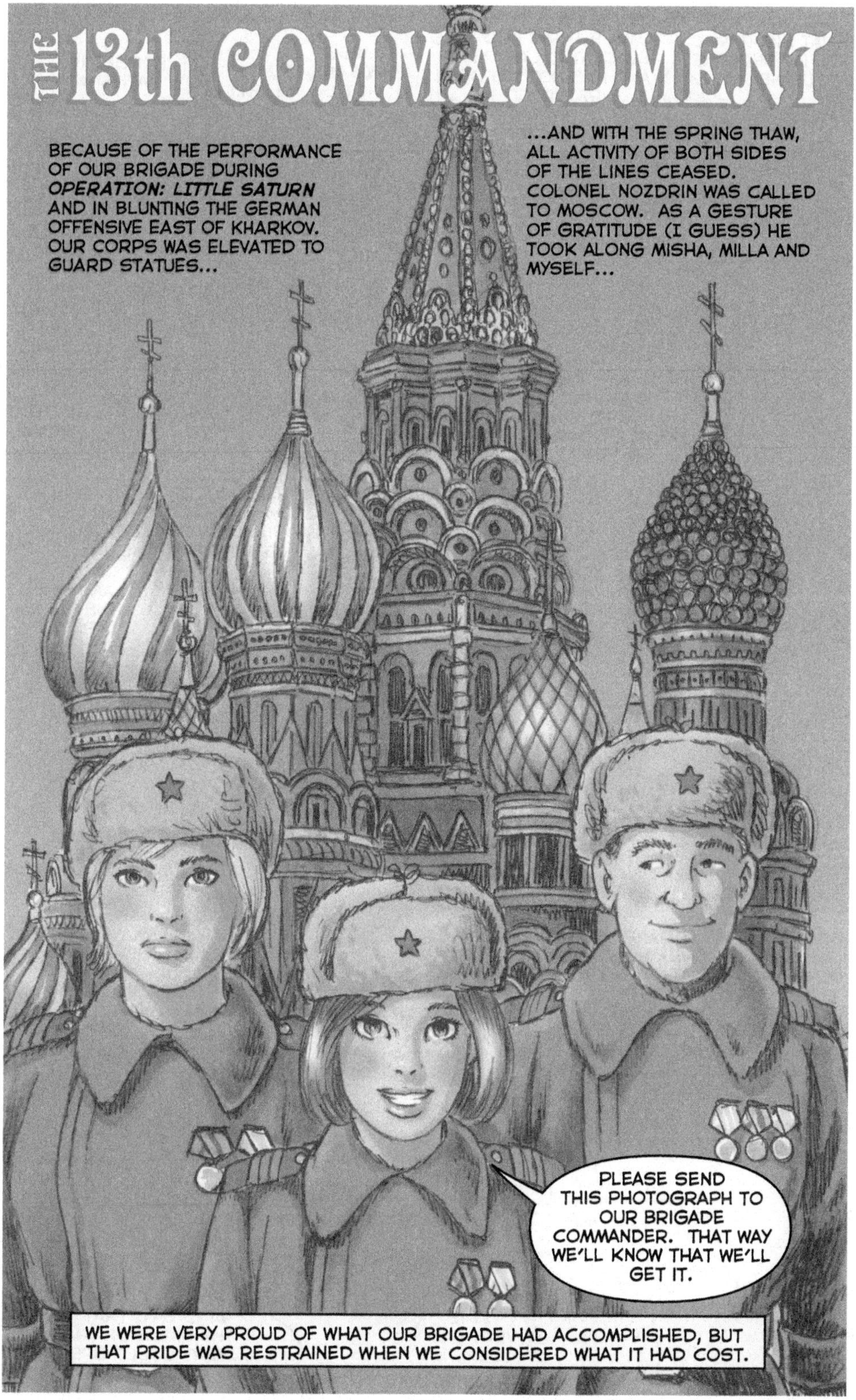
THE 13th COMMANDMENT
BECAUSE OF THE PERFORMANCE OF OUR BRIGADE DURING *OPERATION: LITTLE SATURN* AND IN BLUNTING THE GERMAN OFFENSIVE EAST OF KHARKOV. OUR CORPS WAS ELEVATED TO GUARD STATUES...
...AND WITH THE SPRING THAW, ALL ACTIVITY OF BOTH SIDES OF THE LINES CEASED. COLONEL NOZDRIN WAS CALLED TO MOSCOW. AS A GESTURE OF GRATITUDE (I GUESS) HE TOOK ALONG MISHA, MILLA AND MYSELF...
PLEASE SEND THIS PHOTOGRAPH TO OUR BRIGADE COMMANDER. THAT WAY WE'LL KNOW THAT WE'LL GET IT.
WE WERE VERY PROUD OF WHAT OUR BRIGADE HAD ACCOMPLISHED, BUT THAT PRIDE WAS RESTRAINED WHEN WE CONSIDERED WHAT IT HAD COST.

WELL, MA'AM, WHAT SIGHT WILL YOU BE SHOWING US NEXT?

WE COULD SEE LENIN'S TOMB, BUT HIS BODY WAS EVACUATED LAST YEAR AND HAS NOT YET BEEN RETURNED--

EH, WHO WANTS TO SEE ANOTHER CORPSE, ANYWAY?

MISS! *PLEASE,* NOT SO LOUD!

MILLA!

OH, FORGET IT, KATUSHA.

WE'LL SKIP THAT, MA'AM.

I WISH I COULD MAKE HER SMILE.

I KNOW, MISHA...I KNOW.

NOW, WHAT IS THIS PLACE, MA'AM?

OH, MY GOODNESS! THIS IS LUBYANKA SQUARE--AND THAT LARGE BUILDING ON YOUR LEFT IS LUBYANKA PRISON...

...AND THIS STATUE IS *IRON FELIX!*

SO, THAT IS *FELIX DZERZHINSKY,* FIRST BOSS OF THE *CHEKA*...WELL, WHAT OTHER MONSTERS HAVE STATUES IN THIS CITY?

UHH-- MA'AM, I NOTICE HOW YOU WON'T LOOK AT THE BUILDING...?

NO!

IT IS VERY BAD LUCK...!

MY BROTHER-IN-LAW WAS TAKEN INSIDE THERE IN *1937*...HE *NEVER CAME OUT.* IT IS WHISPERED THEY TORTURED PEOPLE IN THE BASEMENT...

IT IS SAID THAT IF THE WALLS OF THAT BASEMENT COULD SPEAK-- THEY WOULD *SCREAM!*

COMRADES, AS WE ALL KNOW, THE SPRING THAW HAS BROUGHT ALMOST ALL OF OUR OPERATIONS TO A HALT. HOWEVER, OUR INTELLIGENCE UNITS HAVE BEEN WORKING OVERTIME, AND THEIR RESULTS HAVE BEEN EXTRAORDINARY.

CONSEQUENTLY, WE HAVE CONFIRMED THAT HITLER HAS ALREADY ORDERED A MAJOR NEW OFFENSIVE, TO BEGIN NOT BEFORE *MAY 1* OF THIS YEAR.

WE ALREADY KNOW WHERE THE ATTACK WILL OCCUR...

...HERE, AT THE *KURSK SALIENT.* THIS BULGE IN THE LINE EXTENDS ONE HUNDRED MILES INTO GERMAN-OCCUPIED TERRITORY. WE BELIEVE THE BLOW WILL FALL BELOW OREL IN THE NORTH, AND ABOVE BELGOROD IN THE SOUTH.

THEIR INTENT IS TO CUT OFF OUR TROOPS IN THE SALIENT, THEN GO FOR MOSCOW.

AND WE MEAN TO LET THEM TAKE THEIR BEST SHOT. YES! WE WILL NOT INTERRUPT THEIR OFFENSIVE WITH ONE OF OUR OWN. WE SHALL LET THEM BREAK THEIR BACKS UPON OUR DEFENSES--THEN, WE WILL *ATTACK!*

HERE IS WHY THIS WILL WORK: FOLLOWING OUR VICTORY AT STALINGRAD, THE GERMAN TANK FORCES ARE IN TERRIBLE SHAPE. THEY HAVE LESS THAN 500 TANKS ON THE WHOLE FRONT. AS GOOD AS THEY MIGHT BE, THEIR NEW *TIGER TANKS* ARE FAR TOO EXPENSIVE AND TAKE THEM TOO LONG TO QUICKLY CONSTRUCT.

WE ESTIMATE THAT REBUILDING THESE FORCES COULD TAKE THEM UNTIL THE END OF JUNE.

RIGHT NOW, OUR FACTORIES IN THE URALS ARE TURNING OUT *ONE THOUSAND T-34s A MONTH!* SO...THE LONGER IT TAKES THE GERMANS TO PREPARE FOR THEIR OFFENSIVE--

--THE STRONGER *WE* BECOME!

THE SPRING SUN WAS ONLY AN ANTICIPATION AS OUR BRIGADE BEGAN ROLLING TOWARD THE FRONT.

WE LOADED UP OUR FEW REMAINING BATTERED TANKS ON FLATCARS, AND OFF WE WENT...

THIS IS MUCH BETTER THAN OUR TRIP TO THE URALS, *HUH*, MILLA?

WELL, AT LEAST OUR BATHROOM ISN'T AN OIL CAN...!

WE WERE ALL WELL RESTED, AND OUR SPIRITS WERE HIGH.

WE REACHED A POINT WHERE SEVERAL RAILROAD LINES CONVERGED. THERE, RIGHT BEHIND US, WAS A TRAINLOAD OF SHINY NEW GREEN *T-34*s--NOT EXACTLY SOMETHING THAT WOULD EXCITE A YOUNG GIRL, BUT I COULDN'T HAVE BEEN HAPPIER THAN A CHILD WHO'D BEEN GIVEN A NEW DOLL.

SOME OF THESE TANKS HAD NEW FEATURES, WHICH HAD BEEN CAST AT THE SVERDLOVSK PLANT. AND THE *TURRETS--?* WELL...

...THEY REMINDED US OF *COLONEL NOZDRIN.*

THERE WERE NEW RECRUITS, MALE AND FEMALE, WHO NEEDED PROPER TRAINING IN DRIVING AND FIGHTING IN THE TANKS.

EACH TANK *MUST* HAVE A TARPAULIN. THE FIRST TIME IT RAINS--

--YOU'LL FIND OUT *WHY.*

I'D TURNED 18 THAT APRIL AND FELT QUITE THE OLD HAND AS I EXPLAINED HOW TO PATCH AND PRUNE AND STROKE THESE STEEL CREATURES AND HOW TO CURL UP WITH THEM AT NIGHT TO SLEEP.

AND THERE WERE *KV TANKS* AND *76MM* AND *57MM ANTI-TANK GUNS*, AND *KATYUSHA ROCKETS*, AND MOUNTAINS OF AMMUNITION AND SUPPLIES...

...ALL OF IT STREAMING UP FROM SEAPORTS IN PERSIA, BROUGHT IN OR PULLED ALONG BY *STUDEBAKER* AND *GMC* TRUCKS FROM AMERICA.

AND THERE WAS *FOOD*--CANNED VEGETABLES, FRUIT, AND MEAT!

THIS *"SPAM"*...WHAT SORT OF FARM ANIMAL IS IT MADE FROM?

I DUNNO...BUT I'M NOT SURE JEWS CAN EAT IT.

OUR DAYS OF SHORTAGES WERE OVER.

THEN OUR INFANTRY BATTALIONS CAME BACK, FULL OF FRESH NEW FACES, FAMILIAR OLD HANDS--AND SPECIAL ACQUAINTANCES.

WELL, IF IT ISN'T LITTLE TYMOSHENKO! HOW WAS MOSCOW?

WELL, CAPTAIN...IT WAS NOT *KIEV*.

AH, TRULY...NOTHING COMPARES TO *HOME*, DOES IT? I AM SO GLAD TO SEE YOU WELL.

UH... COLONEL NOZDRIN TOLD ME OF WHAT HAPPENED--ABOUT YOUR UNCLE...

PLEASE ACCEPT MY CONDOLENCES.

WELL, WE ALL MUST BEAR OUR LOSSES.

I GUESS IT GIVES US ALL THE MORE REASON TO HATE THE GERMANS.

HIS COMMENT SURPRISED ME.

BUT MY RESPONSE SURPRISED ME *MORE*.

I THINK MILLA FEELS THAT WAY, BUT...NO, I *CANNOT*.

UNCLE TARAS WOULDN'T WANT ME TO THINK LIKE THAT.

HE WASN'T THAT KIND OF MAN.

CAPTAIN KOVCHENKO WAS SILENT FOR A MOMENT, AS IF BAFFLED BY WHAT I SAID.

AH. WELL--MY INFANTRY BATTALION IS BEING PULLED OUT OF THE BRIGADE AND PLACED IN ONE OF THE DEFENSIVE LINES...

...AND COLONEL NOZDRIN'S TANKS ARE ASSIGNED TO THE 5TH GUARD ARMY, IN A RESERVE POSITION.

WHERE WILL *THAT* BE?

LET'S SEE... IT'S A LITTLE TOWN BELOW KURSK...

ITS NAME IS *PROKHOROVKA*.

127

THE WORK IN PREPARING FOR THE GERMAN OFFENSIVE WENT ON WITHOUT A BREAK FOR WEEKS ON END. THOUSANDS OF CIVILIANS, MOSTLY WOMEN AND CHILDREN, WERE FREIGHTED IN TO DIG HUGE ANTI-TANK DITCHES.

MILLIONS OF MINES WERE LAID, AND THOUSANDS OF MILES OF BARBED WIRE STRUNG.

BUNKERS AND PILLBOXES WERE BUILT.

ANTI-TANK GUNS WERE PLACED IN THE FOUNDATIONS OF HOUSES, AND GUNNERY POSITIONS WERE CAMOUFLAGED TO RESEMBLE SOMETHING THAT THEY WERE *NOT*.

AND EVERY SOLDIER WAS SET TO WORK DIGGING TRENCHES FOR THEIR OWN POSITIONS...

REMEMBER WELL THE *13TH COMMANDMENT*...

"IT IS FAR BETTER TO DIG 10 METERS OF *TRENCH*-- THAN A 3-METER *GRAVE*."

MAY PASSED INTO JUNE, AND MORE AND MORE MEN FILED INTO THE LINE. ON EACH SIDE, MORE THAN A MILLION MEN HAD BEEN COMMITTED TO THE BATTLE.

WHEN THE GERMANS FINALLY GOT THE TANKS THAT HAD BEEN PROMISED FROM THEIR FACTORIES, THERE WOULD BE NEARLY 3,500 OF THEM.

THE SOVIETS HAD AROUND 6,000 TANKS.

IN THE SKIES ABOVE KURSK, ALMOST 5,000 AIRCRAFT WOULD BE ENGAGED.

ON *JULY 3,* IT WAS ANNOUNCED THAT WE SHOULD "EXPECT THE GERMAN ATTACK WITHIN THE NEXT THREE DAYS."

ON *JULY 4, 1943,* A SOVIET PATROL WENT OUT IN SEARCH OF SOME "TONGUES."

THEY RETURNED WITH A CAPTIVE SLOVENIAN PRIVATE TAKEN FROM A GERMAN ENGINEER PLATOON.

HE TOLD HIS INTERROGATORS THAT THE ATTACK WOULD BEGIN AT *3AM* THE NEXT MORNING. THE WORD WAS QUICKLY PASSED THROUGH EVERY ECHELON OF THE SOVIET FORCES.

WITHIN THE GERMAN LINES, THE EARLY MORNING HOURS OF *JULY 5* WERE TENSE, BUT QUIET...

BUT RUSSIAN ARTILLERY GOT IN THE FIRST PUNCH--

--AS SOVIET AIRCRAFT HIT THE WAITING GERMAN ASSAULT FORCES!

THIS SHOCK THREW OFF THE GERMAN TIMETABLE SO THOROUGHLY THAT IT WASN'T UNTIL *0430* THAT THEY FINALLY OPENED UP THEIR ARTILLERY...

...BUT OPEN IT UP THEY DID!

THE GERMAN SHELLS FELL AMONG THE FRONTLINE TRENCHES, DRIVING THE RUSSIANS DEEP INTO THEIR WELL-PREPARED SHELTERS.

AT *0500*, BEFORE THE SMOKE COULD CLEAR, THE TANKS AND INFANTRY BEGAN THEIR ADVANCE, C+OMING ON IN BIG, POWERFUL WEDGES OF STEEL AND FIRE.

THE SOVIETS HAD SITUATED THEIR ANTI-TANK DITCHES AND MINEFIELDS TO CHANNEL THE ADVANCE INTO KILLING ZONES--

--WHERE THE UNPROTECTED INFANTRY COULD BE SAVAGELY MAULED.

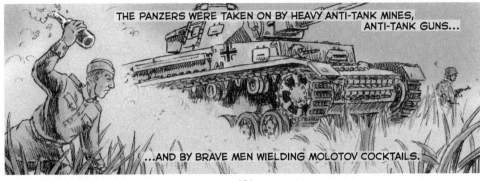

THE PANZERS WERE TAKEN ON BY HEAVY ANTI-TANK MINES, ANTI-TANK GUNS...

...AND BY BRAVE MEN WIELDING MOLOTOV COCKTAILS.

ABOVE THE BATTLEFIELD OF KURSK, HUNDREDS OF PLANES FOUGHT FOR CONTROL OF THE SKIES...

THE GERMAN *JUNKERS 87 "STUKA"* HAD BECOME OBSOLETE AS A DIVE BOMBER...BUT ARMED WITH TWO *37MM ANTI-TANK GUNS--*

--IT MADE A PERFECT "TANK CRACKER."

WITH THIS COMBINED POWER, THE GERMANS WOULD CLOSE IN ON THE RUSSIAN TRENCHES...

132

DURING THE EARLY DAYS OF THIS BATTLE, WE HEARD THE THUNDER AND RUMBLING AND SAW THE CLOUDS OF DUST AND SMOKE. AT NIGHT, THE WESTERN SKIES GLOWED LIKE THE RISING OF AN UNEARTHLY SUN.

WHAT'S THE NEWS, COLONEL?

ON THE NORTHERN SIDE, THE GERMANS HAVE DRIVEN FOUR TO FIVE MILES INTO OUR LINES, BUT ARE STILL PRETTY MUCH CONTAINED...

WELL, THAT'S GOOD...

HERE ON THE SOUTH SIDE, THEY HAVE NOT ADVANCED AS FAR... BUT THEIR PRESSURE SEEMS TO BE MORE CONSISTENT--AND MORE VIOLENT.

WE HAVE KILLED A LOT OF GERMANS-- BUT THEY HAVE KILLED MANY OF US, TOO.

DAY AFTER DAY, THE GERMANS HAMMERED AWAY AT THE SEEMINGLY UNENDING LAYERS OF RUSSIAN TRENCHES, LEAVING IN THEIR WAKE THE SCORCHED HULKS OF THEIR TANKS AND THOUSANDS OF THEIR DEAD.

SOME OF THEIR NEW TANKS THAT WERE SPECIALLY DESIGNED FOR THIS OFFENSIVE PROVED TO BE LESS THAN SATISFACTORY. THE NEW PANTHER COPIED MANY OF THE FEATURES OF THE SOVIET *T-34*, AND EVENTUALLY WOULD BECOME A GREAT FIGHTING VEHICLE.

HOWEVER...

...THE FIRST OUT OF THE FACTORY HAD SO MANY MECHANICAL PROBLEMS THEY BROKE DOWN BEFORE REACHING THE FRONT LINES.

BUT THE REAL JOKE WAS THE *FERDINAND*.

DESPITE ITS POWERFUL *88MM* CANNON, IT HAD NO MACHINE GUNS TO PROTECT IT FROM AN INFANTRY ASSAULT.

A SINGLE BRAVE RED ARMY SOLDIER COULD EASILY BLOW OFF ONE OF ITS TRACKS WITH A GRENADE, AND THEN FINISH IT OFF WITH A MOLOTOV COCKTAIL.

BUT THE *TIGER TANK* RULED THE BATTLEFIELD.

AT OVER 500 METERS DISTANCE, NO RUSSIAN TANK COULD STAND UP AGAINST THE GERMAN TIGER--

--AND GETTING THAT CLOSE ON THE OPEN FIELDS AROUND KURSK WAS A VERY DIFFICULT MANEUVER.

ON *JULY 10*, THE GERMANS REACHED THE *PYSOL RIVER*, THE LAST NATURAL BARRIER TO THEIR LINKUP WITH THE GERMAN FORCES COMING DOWN FROM THE NORTH.

THEY KNEW THE LARGE SOVIET ARMORED FORCES TO THEIR EAST MIGHT POSSIBLY STRIKE THEIR FLANKS, CUTTING OFF THEIR SUPPLIES, COMMAND, AND CONTROL...

RATHER THAN CONTINUE ALONG THEIR AXIS OF ADVANCE, THEY DECIDED INSTEAD TO CHANGE DIRECTION...

...SO THE *2ND SS PANZER CORPS* WHEELED TO THE RIGHT--AND HEADED TOWARD *PROKHOROVKA.*

IN THEIR WAY LAY A LOW, FLAT HILL, GUARDED BY SEVERAL DEEP TANK DITCHES. THE EARTH WAS SEWN WITH MINES AND LACED WITH ENDLESS CURLS OF BARBED WIRE...

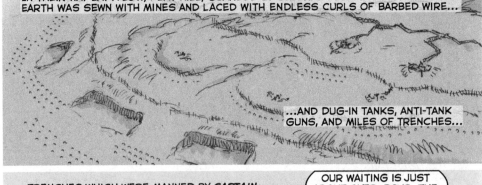

...AND DUG-IN TANKS, ANTI-TANK GUNS, AND MILES OF TRENCHES...

...TRENCHES WHICH WERE MANNED BY *CAPTAIN KOLYA KOLCHENKO'S* INFANTRY BATTALION.

OUR WAITING IS JUST ABOUT OVER, BOYS. THE DEVIL HAS FINALLY ARRIVED.

COMING TO MAKE THEIR ACQUAINTANCE WAS A STEEL WEDGE--TIPPED WITH *TIGER TANKS!*

BEHIND THE TIGERS WERE OTHER GERMAN ARMORED VEHICLES--*PANZER IIIs* AND *IVs*, *STURMGESCHUTZ IIIs*, AND *SCHUTZENPANZERWAGEN 251* HALF-TRACKS--AND OF COURSE, HORDES OF *WAFFEN SS INFANTRYMEN* CLAD IN CAMOUFLAGED SMOCKS!

RUSSIAN MORTAR CREWS WENT RIGHT TO WORK, SEPARATING THE INFANTRY FROM THE PANZERS...

...WITH *DEADLY EFFECT!*

DUG-IN *T-34s* OPENED FIRE ON THE LEAD TANKS...

...ONLY TO HAVE THEIR ROUNDS BOUNCE OFF THE TIGER'S TOUGH SKIN!

NOT WANTING TO WASTE THEIR EFFORTS, THEY WENT AFTER SOFTER TARGETS...

...WITH SOME SUCCESS--

--BUT IT WASN'T LONG BEFORE THE *88s* ENTERED THE DUEL...!

BUT THE BETTER-HIDDEN GUNS HAD FAR GREATER LUCK...

HA! AT UNDER 300 YARDS, THOSE TIGERS BURN AS WELL AS *ANY* TANK!

SEEING THIS SUCCESS, OTHER SOVIET TROOPS SOUGHT THEIR FAIR SHARE OF THE FUN AND GLORY...

HOOO-RAY! FOR KOPELEV!

HOORAY FOR THE *BOY FROM SAMARA!*

THEY CHANGED THEIR APPROACH IN AN ATTEMPT TO AVOID THE HIDDEN ANTI-TANK GUN...

...ONLY TO BE HINDERED BY ANOTHER!

GERMAN INFANTRY POURED OUT OF THEIR HALF-TRACKS...

...CLOSELY COVERED BY THEIR STEEL CHARIOTS.

THE GERMAN ADVANCE WAS VERY COSTLY...

...BUT THEY WERE HAVING SUCCESS.

ONE TANK HELD BACK FROM THE POINT OF THE FRAY--A TIGER WITH A RED BANNER AND THREE ANTENNAS.

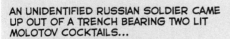

AN UNIDENTIFIED RUSSIAN SOLDIER CAME UP OUT OF A TRENCH BEARING TWO LIT MOLOTOV COCKTAILS...

A GERMAN SERGEANT, PROFESSIONAL AND QUICK TO REACT, GAVE HIM A QUICK BURST OF HIS *MP40*...

WHAAA--!?

--AAAA!!! ⊰WAAAGGHH!⊱

⊰RRRRAAAAWWWW WAAAGGHHH!!⊱

⊰RAAAWGGH!!⊱

⊰YAAARRGHH!!⊱

⊰AAAIIIIEEE!!⊱

141

WITH THAT, AN EARTH-SHAKING, BARELY HUMAN ROAR ISSUED FROM THE RUSSIAN TRENCHES...

...AND WITH IT, MANY OF THE INFANTRYMEN UP ON THE HILL SPILLED OUT ONTO THE INVADERS...

OH, LARYISSA... OH, MY GIRLS...! I COME TO YOU NOW!

WHEN A MAN IS SHOULDER-TO-SHOULDER WITH HIS FRIENDS, HE CAN FACE ODDS THAT WOULD NORMALLY SEEM INSURMOUNTABLE.

HE FEEDS ON THE STRENGTH OF HIS FRIENDS--AND THEY, IN TURN, FEED UPON HIS...

BUT--WHEN ENGULFED BY SMOKE AND DUST AND DARKNESS, IT IS HARD TO TELL WHO IS FRIEND AND WHO IS FOE...

THE ENEMY THAT WAS WEAK AND CONFUSED AND ON THE ROPES SUDDENLY BECOMES STRONG AND PURPOSEFUL AND BELLIGERENT...

...AND THE SINGLE, SOLITARY SOLDIER, WHO BUT A MOMENT BEFORE WAS PART OF THE BRAVE, MOTIVATED "WE"--

--BECOMES THE TIMID, FRAIL "I." *

* HOMAGE TO VASILY GROSSMAN'S LIFE AND FATE.

143

THE COUNTERATTACK, WHICH HAD BEEN VERY COSTLY FOR THE DEFENDERS, FELL APART. BUT IT DID MANAGE TO DEMORALIZE THE GERMANS ENOUGH TO DISSIPATE THEIR STRENGTH. THE ASSAULT ON THE HILL WAS HALTED FOR THE NIGHT.

BY NOW, THE NIGHT OF *JULY 10-11*, THE FULL STRENGTH OF THE *FIFTH GUARD TANK ARMY* WAS MOVING FORWARD--AND WE WERE MOVING WITH IT.

COLONEL NOZDRIN, WE HAVE A MESSAGE FROM THE CORPS COMMANDER...

GENERAL ROTMISTROV IS SETTING UP A FORWARD HEADQUARTERS UP AHEAD, AND HE REQUESTS YOUR PRESENCE.

WE PULLED PAST THE HEAVY MORTAR UNIT TO FIND THE HEADQUARTERS IN AN OLD BARN NEXT TO A WINDMILL.

JUST HANG ON HERE--WE HAVE COMMUNICATIONS SET UP INSIDE, BUT KEEP READY IN CASE I NEED YOU.

WELL, I GUESS THAT LEAVES US OUT OF IT...!

YOU WON'T HEAR *ME* COMPLAIN ABOUT THAT.

WELL, I WILL!

I'M GETTING TIRED OF BEING LITTLE MORE THAN THE BOSS'S CHAUFFEUR!

144

THAT NIGHT, ATOP WHAT I ALWAYS CALLED "KOLYA'S HILL," OUR MEN
DID THEIR BEST TO EVACUATE THE WOUNDED AND PROVIDE
WHAT COMFORT THEY COULD FOR THE DYING...

CAPTAIN KOVCHENKO!

MANY MEN ARE APPROACHING FROM OUR REAR!

IT'S RUSSIAN *PARATROOPS!*

AH! ARE WE EVER GLAD TO SEE YOU, COMRADE!

HOW MANY OF YOUR MEN STILL REMAIN, CAPTAIN?

LESS THAN 300--TODAY'S ATTACK WAS COSTLY...

...AND TOMORROW WILL BE A LOT *WORSE.*

CONTINUE TO HOLD THE CREST. I WILL PLACE MY THREE COMPANIES AROUND YOU.

DOBRY VYECHER, SERGEANT! WOULD YOU PERHAPS LIKE A LITTLE INFANTRY SUPPORT FOR YOUR GUN?

WHY, THANK YOU, LIEUTENANT! IF YOU DON'T MIND, COULD YOU GET YOUR BOYS TO SWEEP ME A CLEAN PATH OUT FRONT?

I NOTICED BEFORE THE SUN SET THAT OUR VIEW WAS BLOCKED BY FASCIST TRASH...!

AT THE CRACK OF DAWN ON *JULY 11*, GERMAN PLANES BEGAN TO RAIN HELL DOWN UPON THE RUSSIAN LINES.

ON THE HILL BELOW, KOLYA, HIS MEN, AND THE NEWLY ARRIVED PARACHUTISTS HUGGED THE BOTTOM OF THEIR TRENCHES AND FOXHOLES...

...WHILE THE BOMBS RATTLED THEM AROUND LIKE DICE IN A TIN CUP.

FROM HIS POSITION ATOP THE CREST OF THE HILL, KOLYA KOVCHENKO COULD SEE THE BATTLE BEGINNING TO TAKE FORM IN THE VALLEY BELOW THEM...

TWENTY-ONE HEAVY *KV TANKS* ROLLED FORWARD TO MEET THE ENEMY. THESE TANKS, ONCE REGARDED AS THE BEST THE RED ARMY HAD, WERE NOW OBSOLETE.

THIS FIGHT WAS TO BE THEIR SWAN SONG.

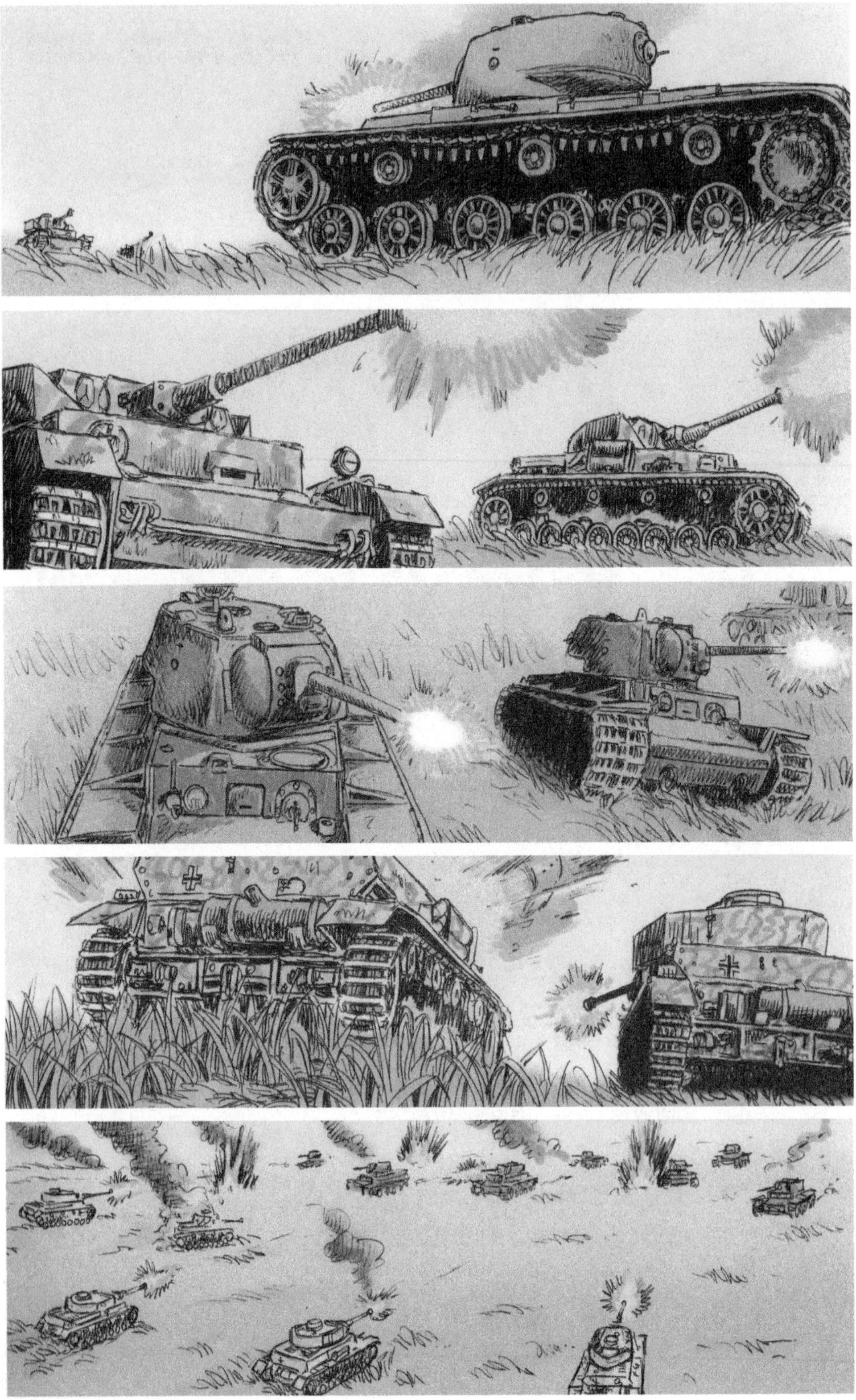

NOW, SUFFICIENTLY REINFORCED, THE GERMAN TANKS ROLLED UP THE HILL...

CAN'T YOU KEEP THAT AMMO COMING ANY FASTER?

I'M SORRY, SERGEANT.

I'M AFRAID THAT I'M THE ONLY LOADER LEFT--

HUH--?! WHAT HAPPENED TO *GRISHIN*?

OH... WAS THAT HIS NAME?

HE WAS HIT JUST A MOMENT AGO...

HE LOOKED KIND OF OLD. HAD YOU KNOWN HIM LONG--?

YES. ALL MY LIFE...

...HE WAS MY FATHER...

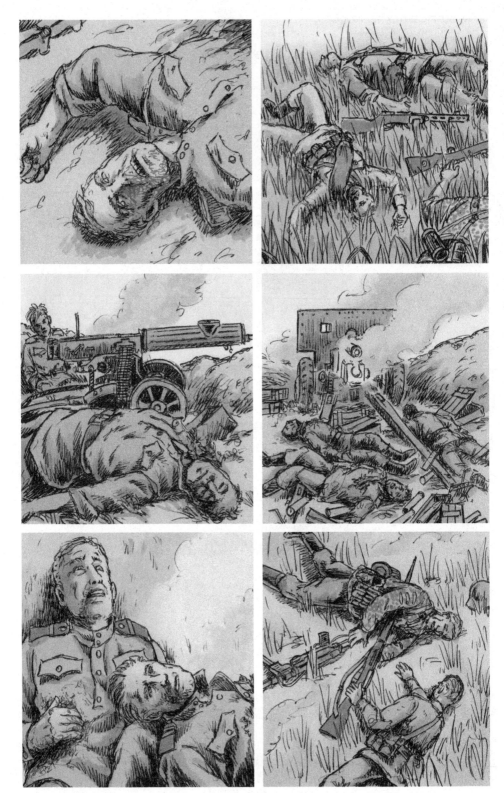

BUT WE WERE STILL WAITING BACK AT LIEUTENANT GENERAL ROTMISTROV'S HEADQUARTERS. FINALLY, *MARSHAL A.M. VASILEVSKY* ARRIVED WITH STRICT ORDERS FROM STALIN HIMSELF. THE DAY WAS WANING BEFORE COLONEL NOZDRIN RETURNED.

I AM TO KEEP MY BRIGADE IN RESERVE UNTIL THE LAST MINUTE...

...SO WE WILL REMAIN HERE UNTIL FURTHER NOTICE.

SO--ARE WE GOING TO *MISS* THIS FIGHT, COLONEL?

DON'T BE RIDICULOUS, MILLA! WE MUST SIMPLY BIDE OUR TIME, FOR STRATEGY'S SAKE.

FROM UP HERE, WE'LL BE ABLE TO SPOT THE GERMANS WITH THE NAKED EYE...

THE SETTING SUN WAS A GREAT RED BALL BURNING ITS WAY THROUGH THE DUST.

SOMEWHERE OUT THERE, A COLOSSAL HAMMER WAS BEATING ON AN ANVIL...

...AND IT WAS DRAWING CLOSER AND CLOSER TO *US*...

150

Katusha

AS THE LEGEND GOES...IN 1295, A LONE PEASANT WANDERING THROUGH A FOREST ON THE BANKS OF THE KHAN BATU RIVER FOUND IT WITHIN THE TRUNK OF A TREE.

IT WAS CALLED THE *KURSK MADONNA.*

A MONASTERY WAS BUILT ON THE SITE OF THE DISCOVERY TO COMMEMORATE THE HOLY EVENT.

WHEN THE BOLSHEVIKS CAME INTO POWER, THEY ENDED THE MONASTIC CREED AND TURNED THE MONASTERY INTO A HOLIDAY CAMP FOR THE *NKVD.*

THE MADONNA WAS *LOST...*

THEN, IN *1943,* THE *NKVD* GAVE THE CHURCH A REPLACEMENT MADONNA--SO THAT THE FAITHFUL COULD PRAY FOR THE VERY SAME GOVERNMENT THAT HAD ENGINEERED ITS PERSECUTION IN THE FIRST PLACE.

HARVEST AT PROKHOROVKA

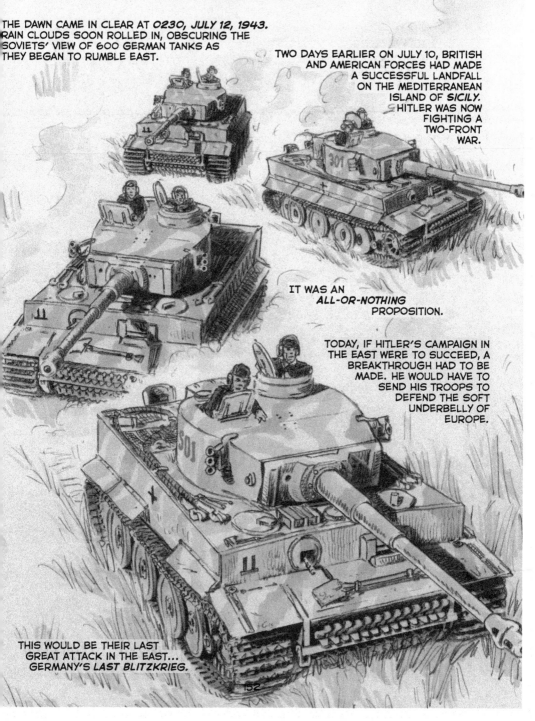

THE DAWN CAME IN CLEAR AT *0230, JULY 12, 1943.* RAIN CLOUDS SOON ROLLED IN, OBSCURING THE SOVIETS' VIEW OF 600 GERMAN TANKS AS THEY BEGAN TO RUMBLE EAST.

TWO DAYS EARLIER ON JULY 10, BRITISH AND AMERICAN FORCES HAD MADE A SUCCESSFUL LANDFALL ON THE MEDITERRANEAN ISLAND OF *SICILY.* HITLER WAS NOW FIGHTING A TWO-FRONT WAR.

IT WAS AN *ALL-OR-NOTHING* PROPOSITION.

TODAY, IF HITLER'S CAMPAIGN IN THE EAST WERE TO SUCCEED, A BREAKTHROUGH HAD TO BE MADE. HE WOULD HAVE TO SEND HIS TROOPS TO DEFEND THE SOFT UNDERBELLY OF EUROPE.

THIS WOULD BE THEIR LAST GREAT ATTACK IN THE EAST... GERMANY'S *LAST BLITZKRIEG.*

WE STOOD IDLE AT THE EDGE OF A FIELD OF SUNFLOWERS, AWAITING COLONEL NOZDRIN'S INSTRUCTIONS. I WALKED BACK ONE HUNDRED YARDS BEHIND US TO THE MORTARS SECTION TO CHECK THEIR FREQUENCY IN CASE WE HAD TO CALL THEM. WHEN I GOT BACK, MISHA WAS ALONE WITH THE TANK...

WHERE IS MILLA?

SHE WENT OUT TO CHECK THE FIELD--IN CASE WE HAVE TO CROSS IT, I GUESS...

...OR MAYBE SHE JUST DOESN'T CARE FOR MY COMPANY.

DON'T TAKE IT PERSONALLY, MISHA--MILLA HAS HER OWN DEMONS. I'VE LEARNED TO ACCEPT HER THE WAY SHE IS.

LET'S SEE...THIS FIELD IS ABOUT 150 YARDS WIDE...

...ABOUT 500 YARDS DEEP...

...WITH THE PSEL RIVER ON THE RIGHT, IRRIGATION CANAL ON THE LEFT...

...A DRY DITCH, ABOUT FOUR FEET DEEP...

THE GERMAN TANKERS HAD STOPPED IN THE HIGH GRASS TO ALSO WAIT. THEY ATE BREAKFAST, NAPPED, AND RELIEVED THEMSELVES, AS THEIR COMMANDERS GATHERED ONE MORE TIME TO GO OVER THE MAPS.

THEN, AT *0830*, THE *LUFTWAFFE* CAME SCREAMING OVERHEAD.

THAT'S *IT!* EVERYBODY MOUNT UP!

AGAIN THE PANZERS WERE ON THE MOVE, WITH THEIR COMMANDERS IN THEIR FANCY BLACK UNIFORMS, SITTING IN THE TURRETS AND SCANNING THE HORIZON FOR THE ENEMY...

SO FAR-- *NOTHING.*

THEN, FROM BEHIND EVERY HILL AND RIDGE, FARMHOUSE AND TREE--THE SOVIET FORCES BEGAN TO EMERGE. JUST A FEW TANKS TO BEGIN WITH...

...BUT SOON, THEY COVERED THE EARTH LIKE ANTS.

THERE WERE LIGHT *T-70*s AMONG THEM, EVEN A HANDFUL OF BRITISH-MADE LEND-LEASE *CHURCHILLS*, BUT THE GREAT MAJORITY WERE *T-34*s. ALL WERE MOVING AT TOP SPEED.

THEIR STRATEGY WAS TO REACH THE GERMANS AS QUICKLY AS POSSIBLE AND MIX IN WITH THEM UP CLOSE, MAKING THE PANZERS LOSE THE ADVANTAGE OF THEIR POWERFUL GUNS AND STRONG ARMOR.

THIS WAS *ROTMISTROV'S FIFTH GUARD TANK ARMY,* ALONG WITH EVERY RESERVE HE COULD MUSTER. THE GERMANS WERE FACING NEARLY 900 TANKS--

--ALL OF WHICH WERE COMMITTED TO THIS GAMBLE.

AS SOON AS THE GERMANS IN THE TIGER TANKS SAW WHAT WAS HAPPENING...

...THEY STOPPED IN THEIR TRACKS AND BEGAN TO TAKE AIM.

THEY FIRED OFF A FEW PREMATURE, WILD SHOTS--

--BUT NOT MANY.

THE GERMANS, WELL TRAINED AND PROFESSIONAL, KEPT THEIR NERVE...

...BUT SO DID *WE!*

MANY OF OUR TANKS WERE LOST BEFORE THEY COULD GET WITHIN LETHAL RANGE OF THE TIGERS...

...BUT ONCE THEY DID, ALL BETS WERE OFF!

ONE SIDE WAS NO DEADLIER THAN THE OTHER.

SOME TIGERS WERE TAKEN OUT AT UNBELIEVABLY CLOSE RANGE...

BUT OTHERS--

--WELL, THEY MAY HAVE FALLEN VICTIM TO THEIR OWN EXCITEMENT.

IN THE CONFUSION, FIVE TIGERS AND TWO HALF-TRACKS SLIPPED DOWN INTO A GULLY THAT CUT DEEP INTO OUR REAR...

CAN YOU SEE ANYTHING?

NOTHING MUCH...

...A LITTLE *FLASH* NOW AND THEN...

--AAH! JUST A *MINUTE--!*

WHAT THE--?!

OH, *MY GOD--* IT'S *TIGERS!* EH... I SEE *FIVE* OF THEM...!

...AND *TWO HALF-TRACKS--* ALL HEADING *OUR WAY!*

THEY'LL REACH THE HEADQUARTERS BEFORE THE COLONEL CAN GET BACK--!

BUT WE *CAN'T STOP SO MANY--!*

EVERYBODY IN THE TANK!

KATUSHA--CAN YOU GET THOSE *MORTAR MEN* ON THE RADIO?

SURE--!

GOOD! WE'RE GOING TO NEED LOTS OF *SMOKE!*

WE TOOK OUR POSITIONS AS MILLA CRANKED UP THE ENGINE...

I'VE GOT AN IDEA...!

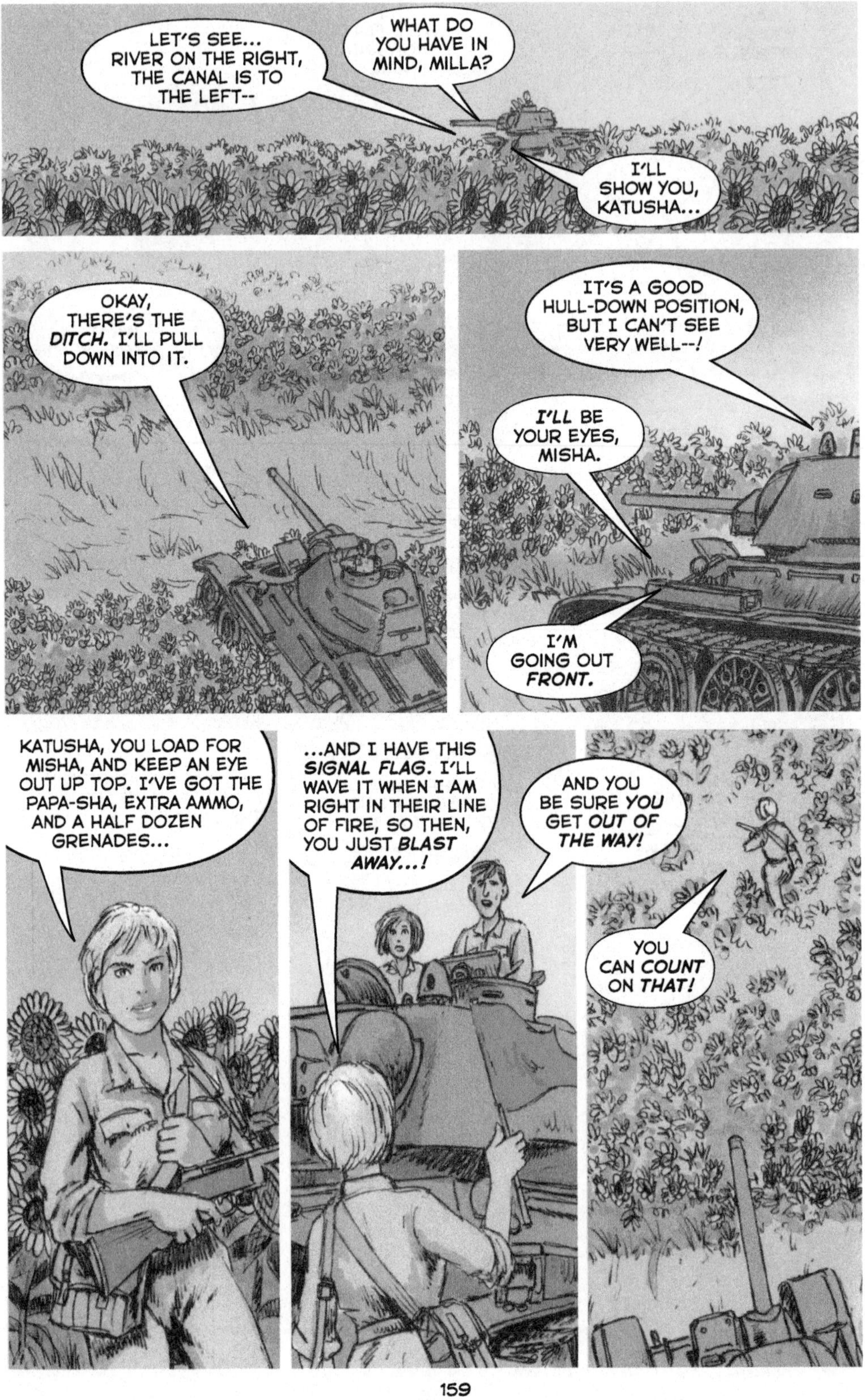
LET'S SEE... RIVER ON THE RIGHT, THE CANAL IS TO THE LEFT--
WHAT DO YOU HAVE IN MIND, MILLA?
I'LL SHOW YOU, KATUSHA...
OKAY, THERE'S THE DITCH. I'LL PULL DOWN INTO IT.
IT'S A GOOD HULL-DOWN POSITION, BUT I CAN'T SEE VERY WELL--!
I'LL BE YOUR EYES, MISHA.
I'M GOING OUT FRONT.
KATUSHA, YOU LOAD FOR MISHA, AND KEEP AN EYE OUT UP TOP. I'VE GOT THE PAPA-SHA, EXTRA AMMO, AND A HALF DOZEN GRENADES...
...AND I HAVE THIS SIGNAL FLAG. I'LL WAVE IT WHEN I AM RIGHT IN THEIR LINE OF FIRE, SO THEN, YOU JUST BLAST AWAY...!
AND YOU BE SURE YOU GET OUT OF THE WAY!
YOU CAN COUNT ON THAT!

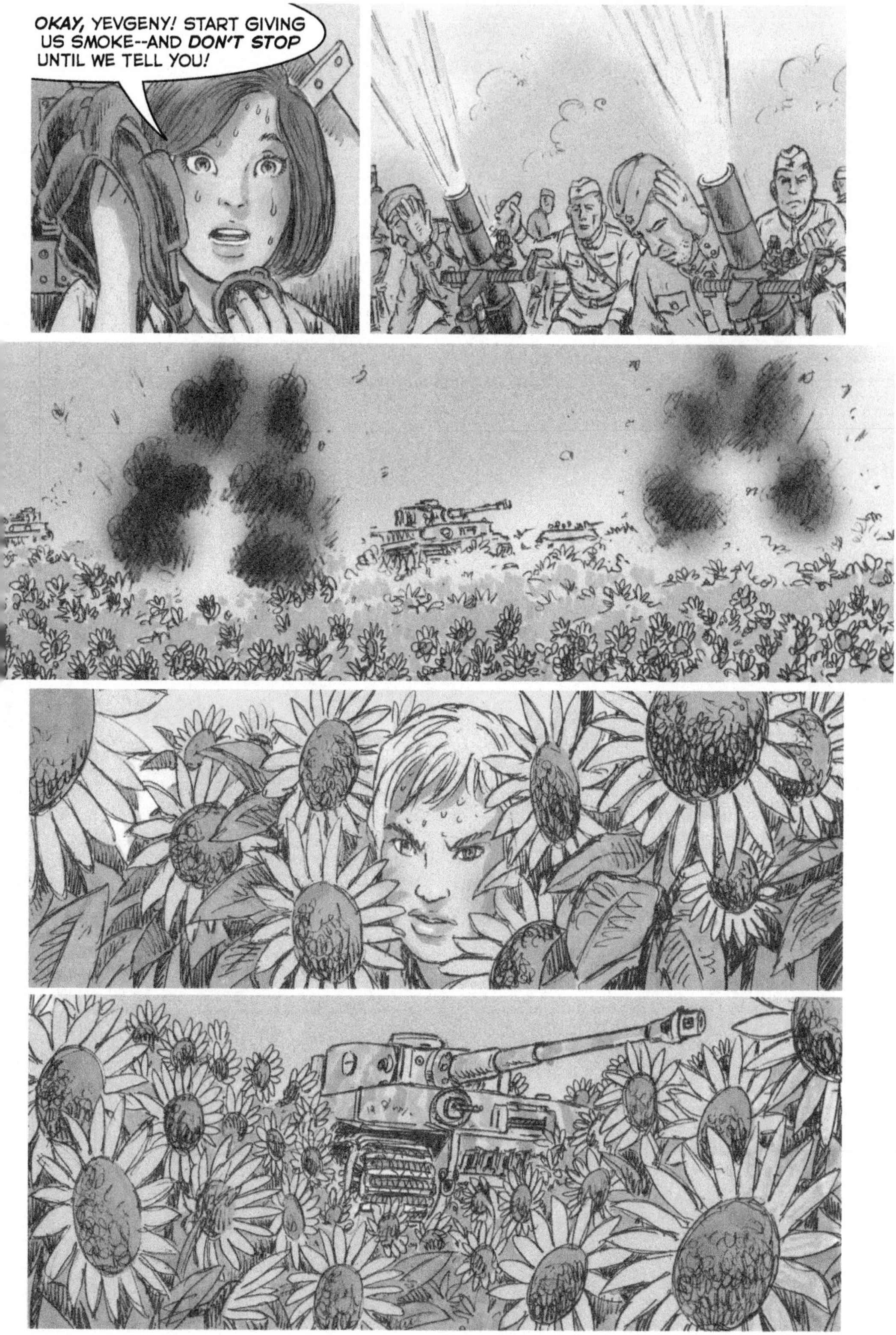
OKAY, YEVGENY! START GIVING US SMOKE--AND DON'T STOP UNTIL WE TELL YOU!

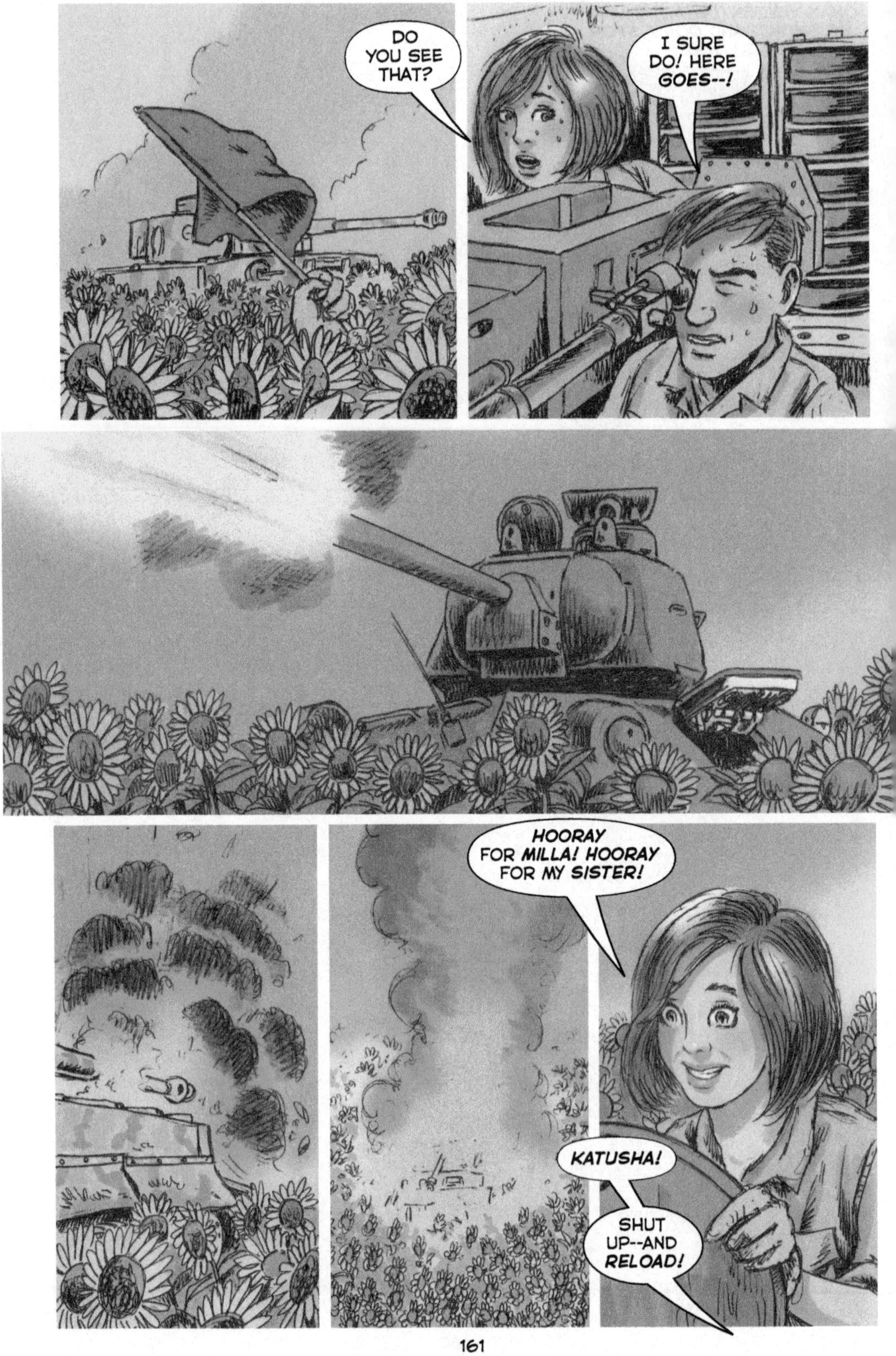
DO YOU SEE THAT?
I SURE DO! HERE GOES--!
HOORAY FOR MILLA! HOORAY FOR MY SISTER!
KATUSHA!
SHUT UP--AND RELOAD!

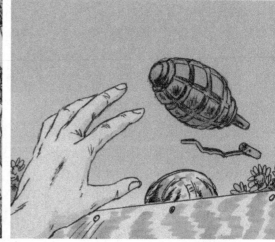

AAAIIIEEE!!
MEIN GOTT!

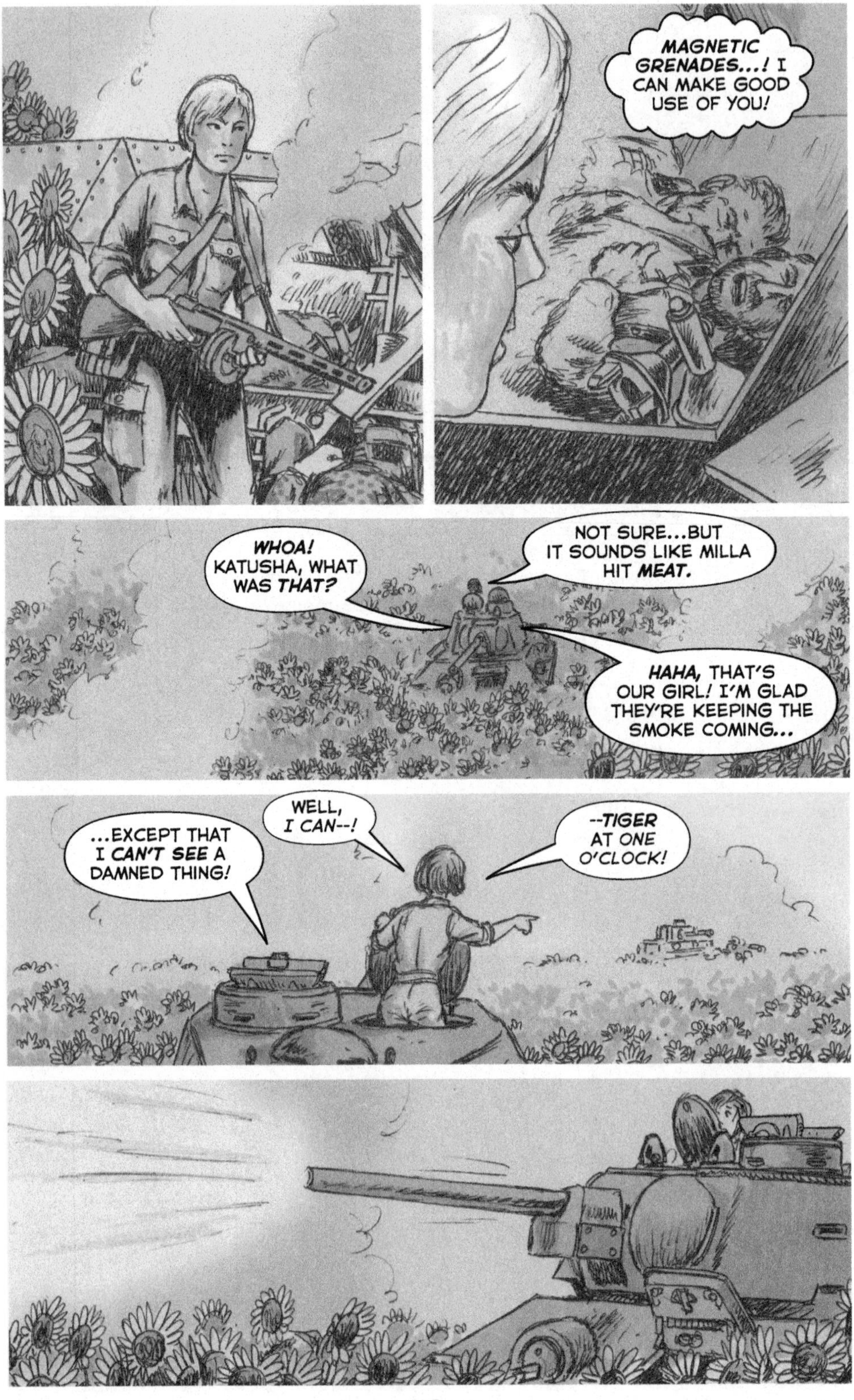
MAGNETIC GRENADES...! I CAN MAKE GOOD USE OF YOU!
WHOA! KATUSHA, WHAT WAS THAT?
NOT SURE...BUT IT SOUNDS LIKE MILLA HIT MEAT.
HAHA, THAT'S OUR GIRL! I'M GLAD THEY'RE KEEPING THE SMOKE COMING...
...EXCEPT THAT I CAN'T SEE A DAMNED THING!
WELL, I CAN--!
--TIGER AT ONE O'CLOCK!

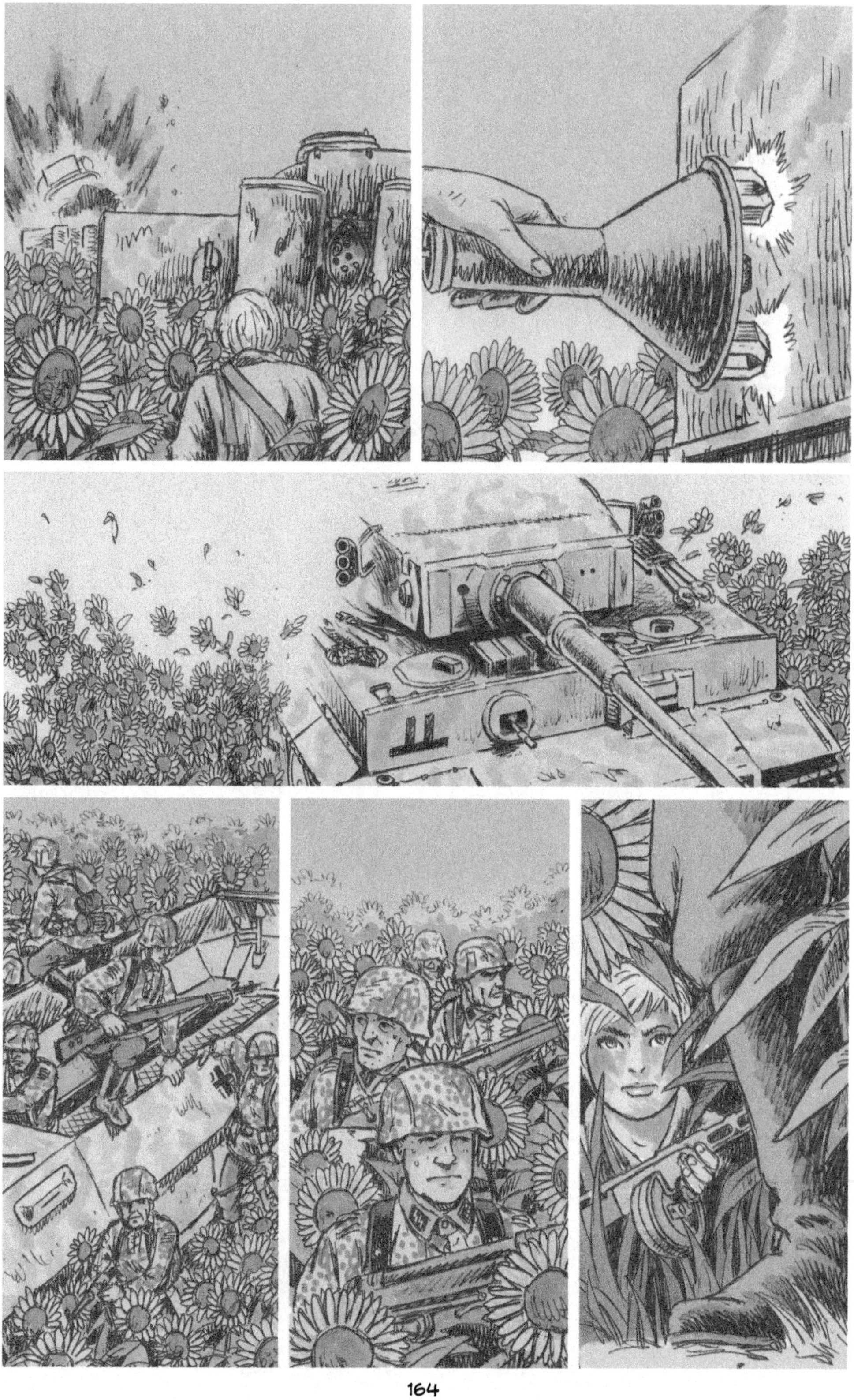

:AWK!:

:OOOF!:

:RAARR-AGHH!:

:AAGGHHK!:

165

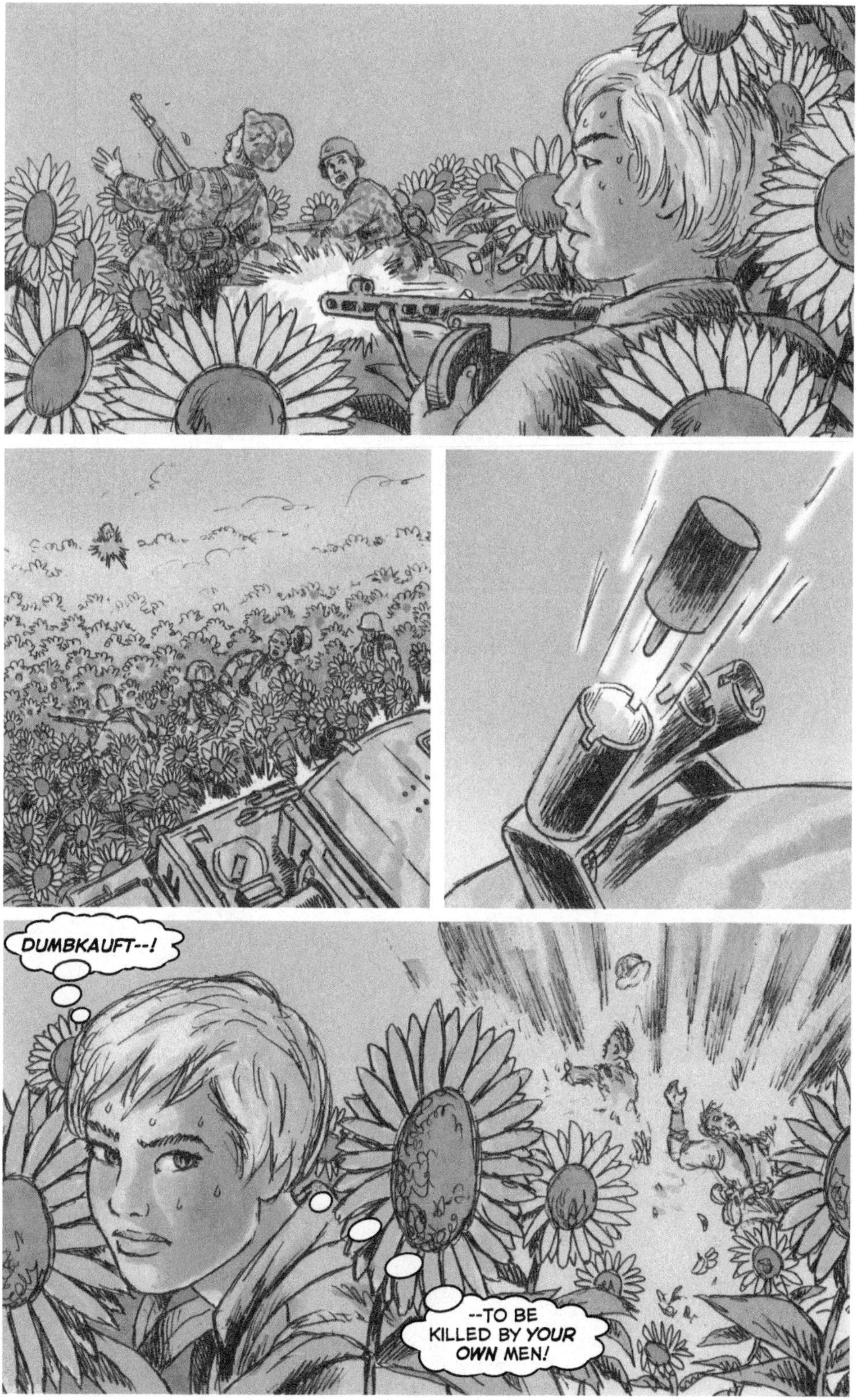
DUMBKAUFT--!
--TO BE KILLED BY YOUR OWN MEN!

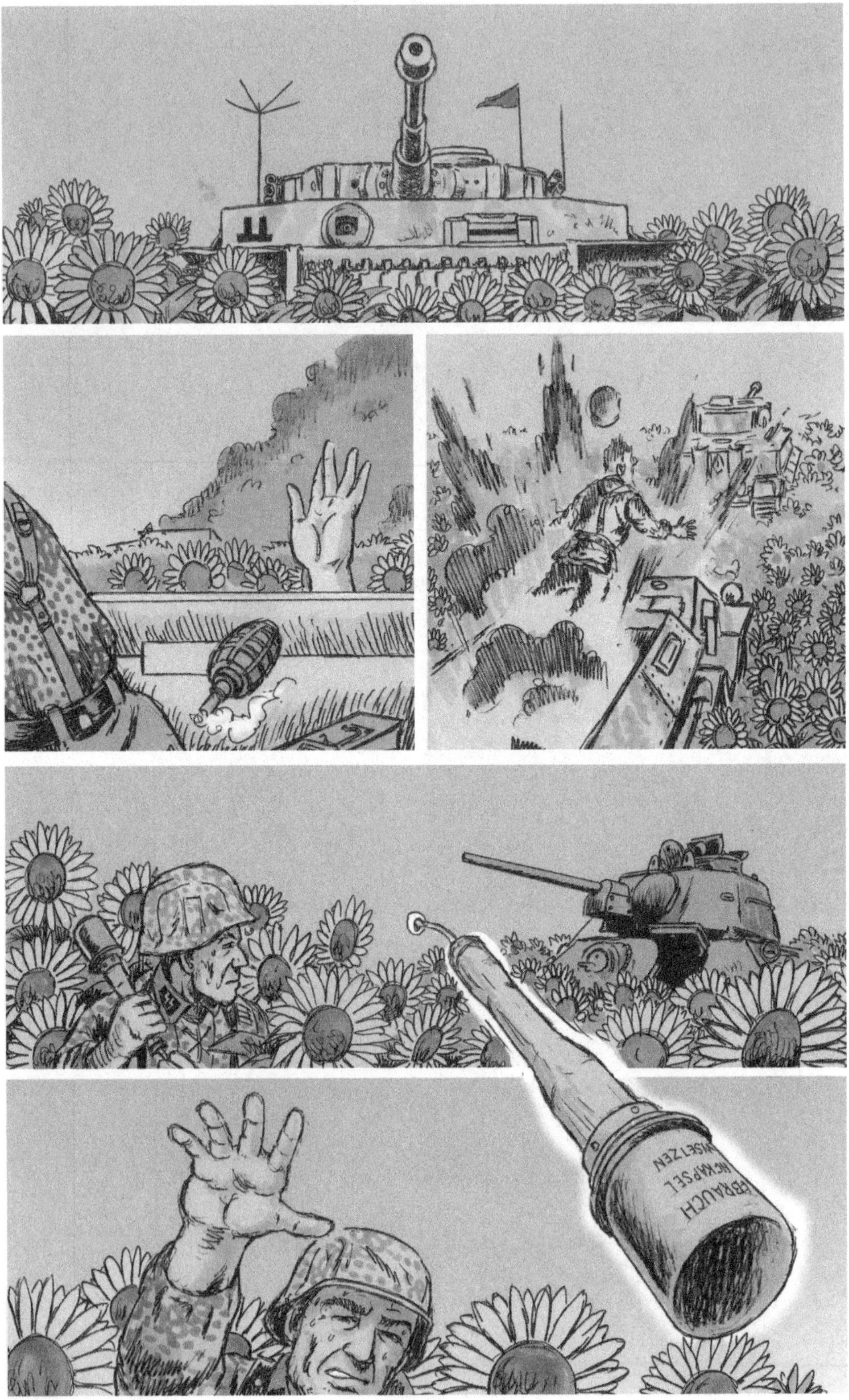

THE GRENADE BOUNCED OFF OUR TANK--

--BUT IT DIDN'T MISS US BY *FAR ENOUGH!*

AAAGGHH!

KATUSHA--! I'M HIT BAD--IN BOTH LEGS!!!

AAH!!

HANG *ON,* MISHA!

MISHA! ANOTHER *TIGER--* RIGHT AT *TWO* O'CLOCK--!

YOU HIT THE TURRET RING! YOU'RE *RELOADED*, MISHA...!

...YOU'VE *GOT* TO HOLD ON!

YOU HIT THE TRACK!

BUT-- THEY'RE STILL IN THE FIGHT, MISHA...

...MISHA?

⌐URRGHH⌐

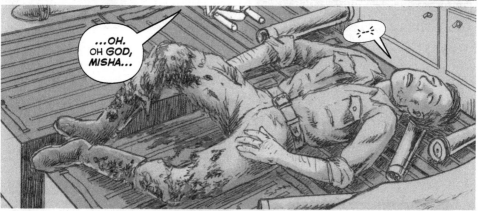

...OH. OH *GOD*, MISHA...

⌐--⌐

I IMMEDIATELY CLIMBED INTO THE GUNNER'S SEAT...

LET'S SEE-- I *DID* RELOAD. DIDN'T I--?

⌐*AAAAUGH!*⌐

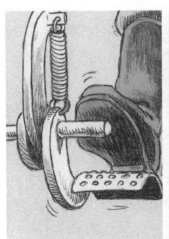

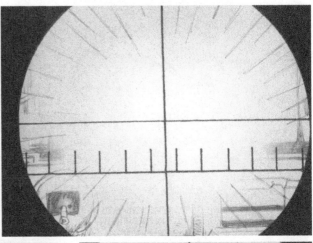

I WAS SUDDENLY AWARE OF THIS LOUD RINGING IN MY EARS--BUT I HAD NO IDEA WHERE IT COULD BE COMING FROM...

...THEN I REALIZED THAT WHAT WAS CAUSING IT WAS THE *DEAD SILENCE!*

I HAD MANAGED TO SCORE A HIT--

--RIGHT IN THE TIGER'S *GUN BARREL!*

SUDDENLY, I WASN'T ALONE--COLONEL NOZDRIN CAME ROARING UP IN HIS *GAZ*, AND THE MORTAR MEN CAME RUNNING UP, EMBARRASSED LOOKS PLAYING ACROSS THEIR FACES.

KATUSHA--!

SORRY, LITTLE TYMOSHENKO--! WE RAN OUT OF SMOKE SHELLS!

THAT'S ALL RIGHT--BUT THERE IS A *WOUNDED MAN* IN HERE...!

THERE, BOVA, YOU DID *WELL*. IT'S GOING TO BE ALL RIGHT...

÷OHHH÷

BUT-- WHERE IS *MILLA?*

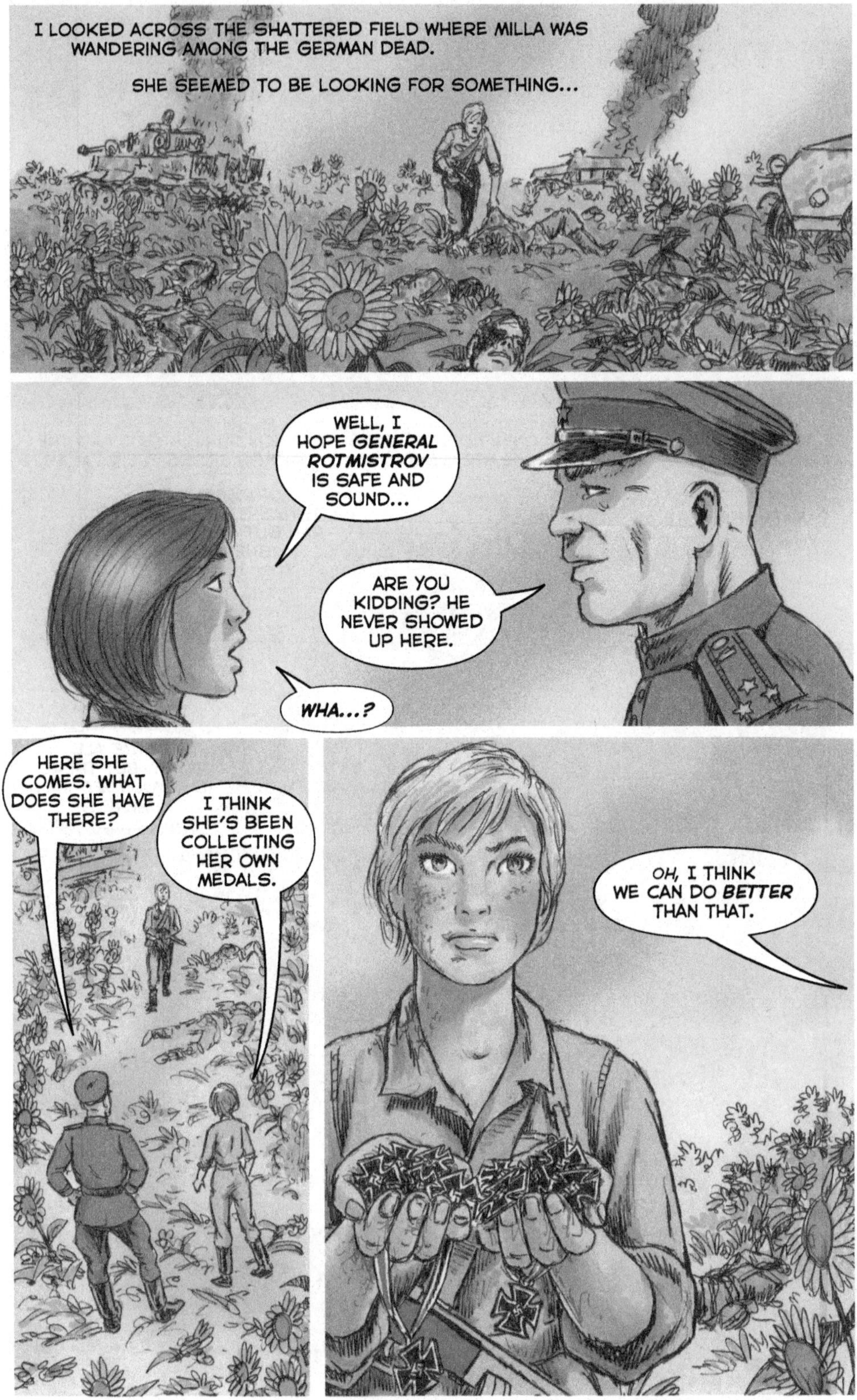
I LOOKED ACROSS THE SHATTERED FIELD WHERE MILLA WAS WANDERING AMONG THE GERMAN DEAD.
SHE SEEMED TO BE LOOKING FOR SOMETHING...
WELL, I HOPE GENERAL ROTMISTROV IS SAFE AND SOUND...
ARE YOU KIDDING? HE NEVER SHOWED UP HERE.
WHA...?
HERE SHE COMES. WHAT DOES SHE HAVE THERE?
I THINK SHE'S BEEN COLLECTING HER OWN MEDALS.
OH, I THINK WE CAN DO BETTER THAN THAT.

THE GROUND AROUND PROKHOROVKA WAS LITTERED WITH THE MANGLED BODIES OF THE DEAD AND THE TWISTED, BURNING HULKS OF TANKS...

THE GERMANS HAD INFLICTED GREAT DAMAGE UPON US.

BUT THEY HAD NOT BROKEN THROUGH.

THEY HAD DONE THEIR WORST...AND HAD *FAILED.* GERMAN TROOPS WOULD NEVER AGAIN ADVANCE INTO RUSSIA.

AND ONCE THE RED ARMY, NOW THE LARGEST FORCE EVER KNOWN IN WAR, BEGAN TO MOVE...

...IT WOULD NEVER STOP.

OUR FORCES BURST FORTH LIKE A COILED SPRING. ON *AUGUST 5*, MEN CLAD IN DUSTY BOOTS AND SUN-BLEACHED SHIRTS ENTERED THE CITY OF *OREL*...

ON THAT SAME DAY, THEY LIBERATED *BELGOROD*.

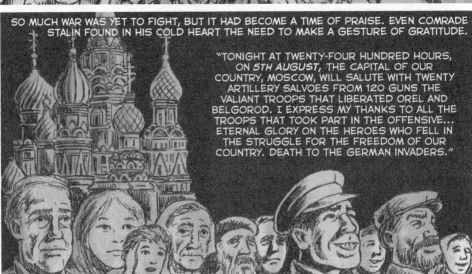

SO MUCH WAR WAS YET TO FIGHT, BUT IT HAD BECOME A TIME OF PRAISE. EVEN COMRADE STALIN FOUND IN HIS COLD HEART THE NEED TO MAKE A GESTURE OF GRATITUDE.

"TONIGHT AT TWENTY-FOUR HUNDRED HOURS, ON *5TH AUGUST*, THE CAPITAL OF OUR COUNTRY, MOSCOW, WILL SALUTE WITH TWENTY ARTILLERY SALVOES FROM 120 GUNS THE VALIANT TROOPS THAT LIBERATED OREL AND BELGOROD. I EXPRESS MY THANKS TO ALL THE TROOPS THAT TOOK PART IN THE OFFENSIVE... ETERNAL GLORY ON THE HEROES WHO FELL IN THE STRUGGLE FOR THE FREEDOM OF OUR COUNTRY. DEATH TO THE GERMAN INVADERS."

175

THERE WAS INDIVIDUAL PRAISE, TOO...

OUR BRIGADE HAD AGAIN DONE WELL.

COLONEL RUSLAN NOZDRIN WAS COMMENDED AND DECORATED.

HE ACCEPTED HIS AWARD WITHOUT COMMENT OR EXPRESSION.

CAPTAIN NIKOLAI KOVCHENKO AND THE MEN WHO SURVIVED THE BATTLE FOR *HILL 221* WERE PROPERLY REWARDED. KOLYA HAD AGAIN BEEN WOUNDED, WHICH AMOUNTED TO A FEW NICKS AND CUTS.

I RECEIVED A MEDAL FOR OUR ACTION IN THE SUNFLOWER FIELD. IT WAS NICE, AND IT MADE ME FEEL GOOD.

BUT IT WAS NOT *MY* AWARD THAT GAVE ME THE MOST PRIDE...

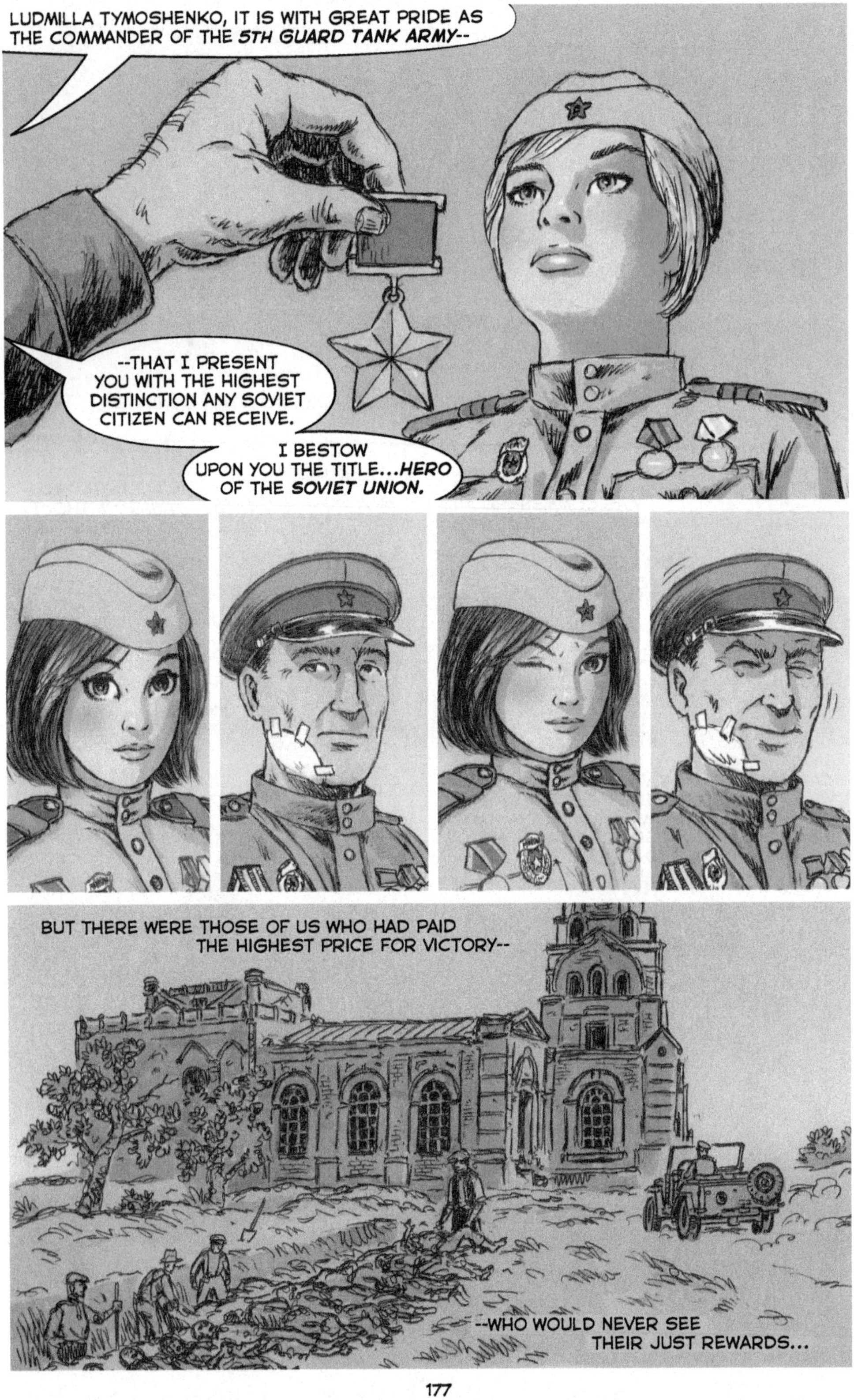
LUDMILLA TYMOSHENKO, IT IS WITH GREAT PRIDE AS THE COMMANDER OF THE *5TH GUARD TANK ARMY*--
--THAT I PRESENT YOU WITH THE HIGHEST DISTINCTION ANY SOVIET CITIZEN CAN RECEIVE.
I BESTOW UPON YOU THE TITLE...*HERO* OF THE *SOVIET UNION.*
BUT THERE WERE THOSE OF US WHO HAD PAID THE HIGHEST PRICE FOR VICTORY--
--WHO WOULD NEVER SEE THEIR JUST REWARDS...

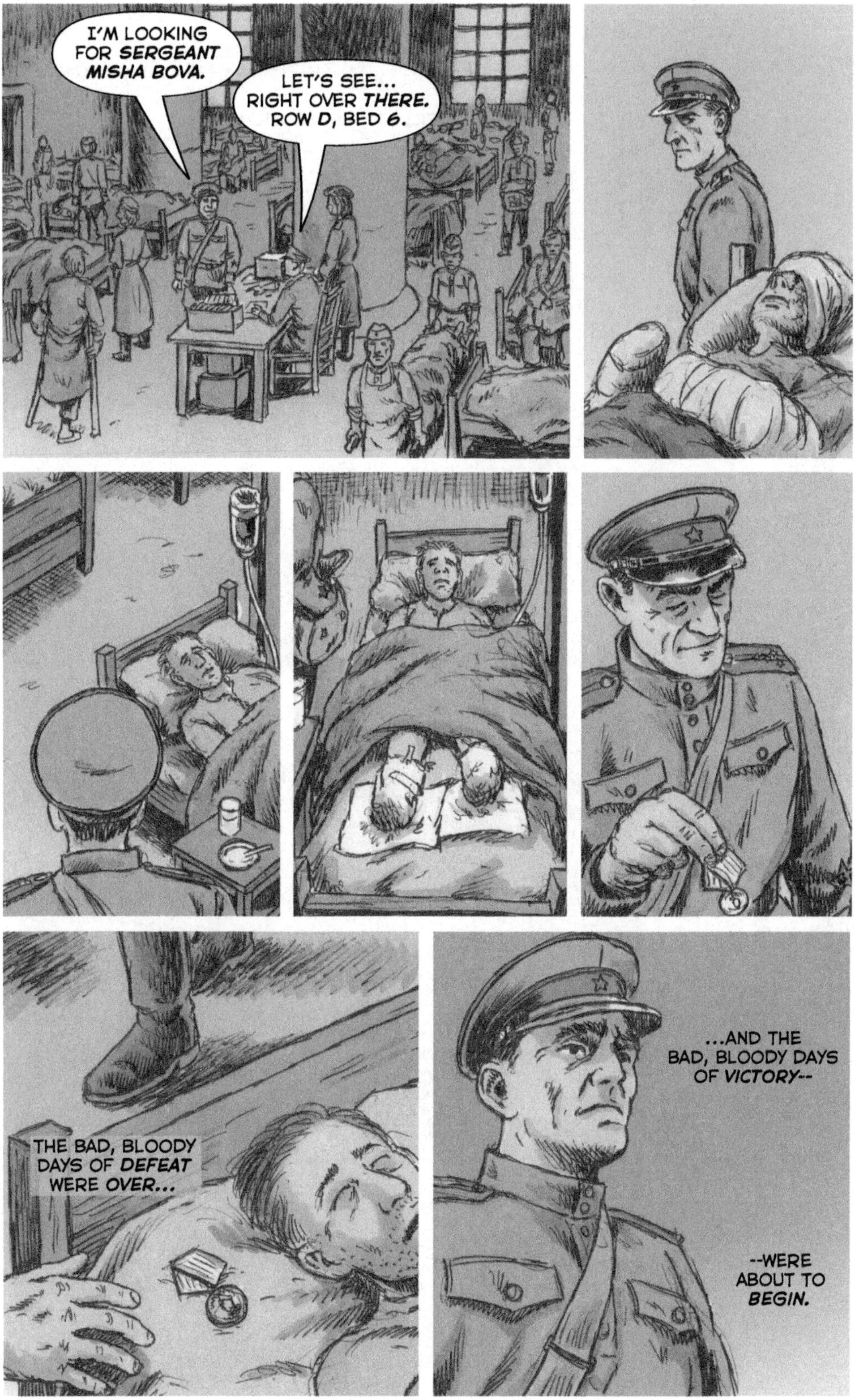
I'M LOOKING FOR SERGEANT MISHA BOVA.
LET'S SEE... RIGHT OVER THERE. ROW D, BED 6.
THE BAD, BLOODY DAYS OF DEFEAT WERE OVER...
...AND THE BAD, BLOODY DAYS OF VICTORY--
--WERE ABOUT TO BEGIN.

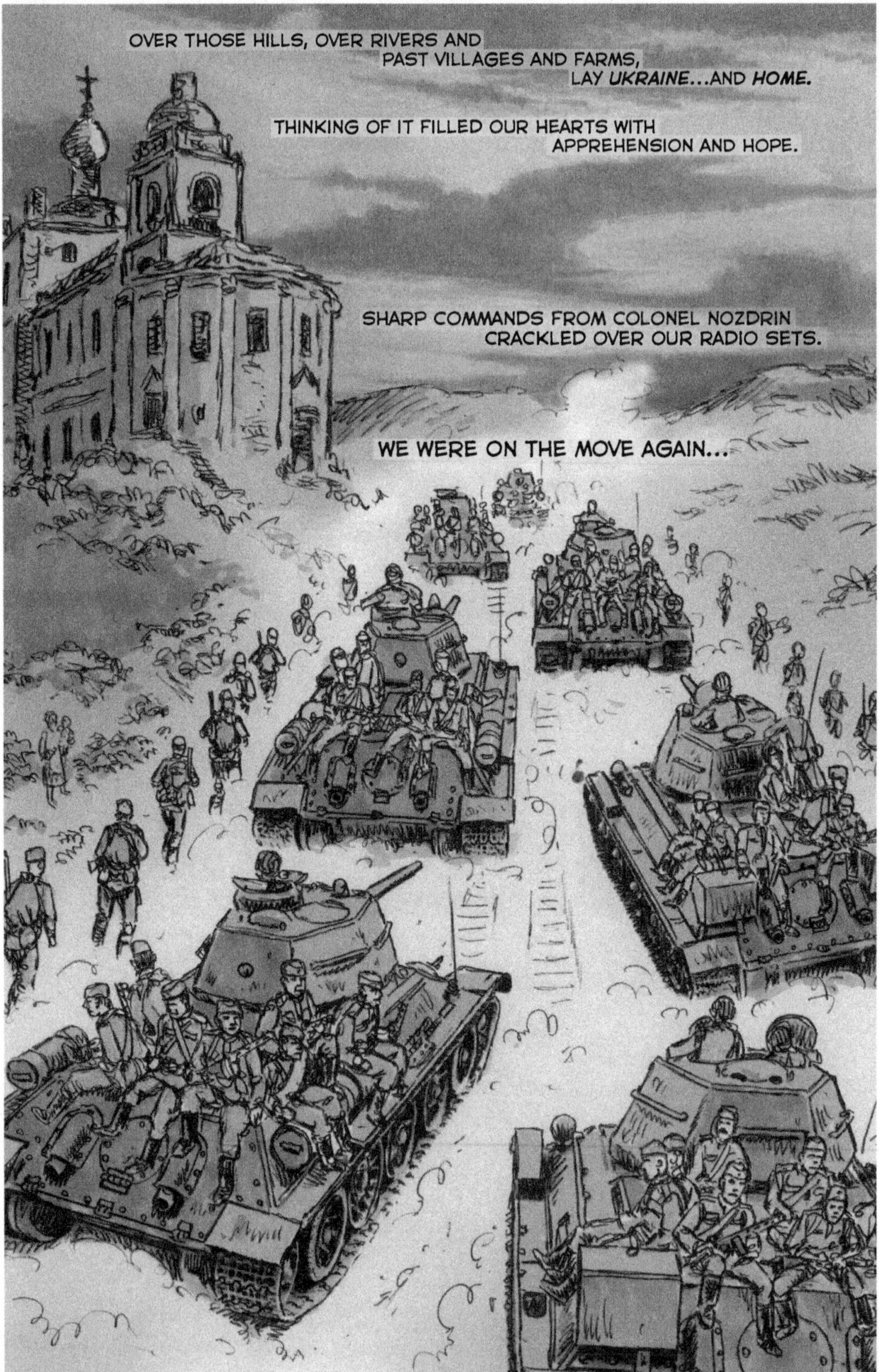
OVER THOSE HILLS, OVER RIVERS AND PAST VILLAGES AND FARMS, LAY *UKRAINE*...AND *HOME.*
THINKING OF IT FILLED OUR HEARTS WITH APPREHENSION AND HOPE.
SHARP COMMANDS FROM COLONEL NOZDRIN CRACKLED OVER OUR RADIO SETS.
WE WERE ON THE MOVE AGAIN...

THE EASTERN FRONT
SOUTH WESTERN RUSSIA, 1942-1943

CPSIA information can be obtained
at www.ICGtesting.com
Printed in the USA
LVOW02s2024050516

486908LV00006B/13/P